HOT PURSUIT
ON THE HIGH SEAS

PETER REESE DOYLE

PUBLISHING

Colorado Springs, Colorado

HOT PURSUIT ON THE HIGH SEAS

Copyright © 1994 by Peter Reese Doyle. All rights reserved.

International copyright secured.

Library of Congress Cataloging-in-Publication Data
Doyle, Peter Reese, 1930-

    HOT PURSUIT ON THE HIGH SEAS / Peter Reese Doyle.

    p. cm—(Daring Family adventures ; bk 5)

    Summary: Penny and Mark Daring and their friend David Curtis
tangle with thieves over stolen treasures of Greece.

    ISBN 1-56179-259-4

    [1. Adventure and adventurers—Fiction. 2. Greece—Fiction.

    3. Christian life—Fiction. 4. Brothers and sisters—Fiction.]

    I. Title. II. Series: Doyle, Peter

Reese, 1930-   Daring Family adventures : bk. 5.

PZ7.D777 Ho 1994

[Fic]—dc20

                   94-14347

                   CIP

                   AC

Published by Focus on the Family Publishing, Colorado Springs,
Colorado 80995.

Distributed in the U.S.A. and Canada by Word Books, Dallas, Texas.

No part of this publication may be reproduced, stored in a retrieval sys-
tem, or transmitted in any form or by any means—electronic,
mechanical, photocopy, recording, or otherwise—without prior permis-
sion of the copyright owner.

Editor: Etta Wilson
Designer: James A. Lebbad
Cover Illustration: Ken Spengler

Printed in the United States of America
94 95 96 97 98 99 / 10 9 8 7 6 5 4 3 2 1

For

Austin Kelvin Doyle
(1898-1970)
Admiral, United States Navy

A model of integrity and courage.

CONTENTS

CHAPTER 1

TREASURES OF ANCIENT GREECE

The whole nation came to a halt. In homes, in shops, in offices, and in warehouses—wherever people could find a television set—work ceased. Even the schools had suspended their normal classes so that children and their teachers could watch the dramatic event by television.

And what a dramatic event it was: the transfer of some of Greece's most priceless ancient treasures from the National Archaeological Museum of Athens to a ship that would take them to be displayed in the British Museum of London.

Tens of millions of people throughout Europe watched their TV sets in awe as the assembled cameras focused on the museum. Untold millions saw the city officials gathered behind the assistant director of the museum as that commanding figure described the irreplaceable historic treasures that Athens was lending to the British Museum.

Built by Ludwig Lange in 1860, the National Archaeological Museum of Athens contains the finest collection of Greek art in the world. The riches within its galleries defy monetary calculation, not only because of their priceless workmanship but also because of the history the treasures represent.

The museum's director was consequently one of the most important men in Athens. However, a conference of museum directors in Sweden had forced him to delegate to his trusted assistant, Andropous Lycenus, all of the arrangements for lending some of the museum's treasures to the British Museum. So the director hadn't concerned himself with the complex security arrangements his assistant had devised. He wasn't present at the press conference held at the loading entrance of the museum. He wasn't there to witness the guarded transfer of the irreplaceable Greek artifacts from the museum to the gleaming white van that would take them to the waiting ship, and from there to London.

He didn't see the police cars and motorcycles that both preceded and followed the van when it arrived at the museum. Nor did he witness the elaborate signing in full view of the television cameras for the twelve barrels containing the treasures. He did not see their removal from the storage room of the museum to the waiting vehicle. Why should the director concern himself with such details when he had an assistant director of the caliber of Andropous Lycenus?

Taller than the average Greek, full-bodied and muscular, of swarthy complexion, Andropous Lycenus had a long, distinguished face and a magnificent moustache. He was an orator. When dealing with the press, he was both gracious and eloquent. From the museum's point of view, he was a public relations dream come true!

He stood before the assembled people and, through the wonders of television, before much of Europe. Elegant in white suit and blue silk tie, he seemed to sum up in his very person the historic glory of his nation. His bearing captivated his audience. The transfer of the priceless art treasures had been well publicized, and millions were glued to their tele vision sets to witness the event. Shops and offices throughout the country came to a standstill; all Greece was watching.

Andropous Lycenus stalked majestically before the barrels containing the treasures. He stood elegantly beside the platform as the barrels were loaded into the van, and he signed with a flourish the documents releasing the art into the hands of the company responsible for the shipment to London.

His speech—apparently informal but actually carefully crafted—lived up to the expectations of the press. Modestly giving credit to his director, he in fact drew full attention to himself. He spoke confidently and directly into the assembled battery of microphones and television cameras.

All Greece swelled with pride as Lycenus spoke. The history of the nation passed through the minds of his fellow citizens as he portrayed the great glories of their past. Then he described with brief eloquence some of the outstanding golden treasures that had just been loaded into the van.

What treasures these were, he told them! The famous King's Gold Mask from the year 1580 B.C.; the Warrior's Vase from the year 1200 B.C.; the gold cups, gold vases, gold jewelry—priceless objects all! He paused; then he told of the two golden cups of Sparta, dating from the fifteenth century B.C.!

The whole exhibit was contained in a dozen carefully packed barrels. Not a large exhibit, but a noble one, a majestic one, an exhibit to make a nation proud! It made Greece proud that day.

The confident orator pictured the thrill that would sweep the international crowds when they gazed upon these mementoes of Greek glory. Then Lycenus thanked the citizens of Greece for the privilege of serving them in his capacity as assistant to the director of the famous museum. And he choked with emotion as he admitted to the pride and the privilege of being a Greek. Even the reporters had tears in their eyes when he finished.

Andropous Lycenus turned with a flourish, waved his hand gracefully like the orators in ancient Greek legends, and stood at grave attention while the caravan with Greece's artistic treasures moved away from the curb.

The massed cameras turned toward the white van as the caravan of police motorcycles and squad cars moved slowly into the boulevard along with it and drove toward the port where the treasure would be loaded for transport by ship bound to London. Somehow people knew that they were watching history move through time and space to inspire another generation by reminding them of great deeds done in the past.

Gradually the van with its escort moved out of sight. Lycenus and his aides returned to their offices; the TV crews packed up their equipment and moved away; the crowd dispersed. People throughout Greece went back to work.

Consequently, there was no one present an hour later when an unmarked gray van drove to the same loading dock of the museum. The museum door opened as if by signal, and two workers proceeded to bring out a dozen barrels and load them into the waiting vehicle.

The driver reentered the van and started the engine. The vehicle pulled out from the curb, entered the flow of traffic, and disappeared from view.

CHAPTER 2

ATHENS

Mark and Penny Daring and their friend David Curtis were beside themselves with excitement! The Olympic Airways jet that had brought them from Paris to the capital of Greece had just landed. From the air they'd seen part of the famous Acropolis, and they couldn't wait to tour the glories of ancient architecture that represented the origins of Western civilization.

Jim Daring, Mark and Penny's father, had business for several days in Athens, and he'd brought the three teens with him on this trip. David had come to visit the Darings at their home station in Africa several weeks before, thinking they would have a fun, but quiet visit. Instead, a series of exciting adventures had taken the three teenagers to Egypt, then to Paris, then to Carcassone in southern France—and now to Greece!

Mark Daring was 17, five feet eleven inches tall, with a powerful build. A year older than his sister, Penny, he had a broad, open face, blond hair like his father, and friendly blue eyes.

Penny, a slender girl with light brown hair, brown eyes,

and dimples in her cheeks, was a serious photographer. She planned to take lots of pictures of the spectacular remains of Greek history.

David Curtis was well-muscled like Mark, but taller by two inches, and lean. Brown eyes looked out from a long face under his thick, dark brown hair.

The three teens were great friends. They'd been through some remarkable adventures together the past four weeks, and they were eagerly looking forward to their visit to Greece.

Leaving the airport with Mr. Daring, they hailed a taxi to take them to the suburban home of his friend, where they would stay during their visit.

"Alexander Spirodes is a remarkable guy," Mr. Daring told them as the taxi drove madly through the city's congested streets. "He's a brilliant businessman, who made his money in shipping. He wants to finance part of the work Paul Froede and I are doing in Egypt, which is why he asked me to visit. But he has many other interests as well. You'll be amazed when you see what he has in his home."

Mr. and Mrs. Spirodes were waiting for them when the taxi pulled through the gate, drove up the long driveway, and stopped before their home. The two-story building in the classic style had six wide Doric columns gracing the front. Their perfect proportions obscured the real dimensions of the house.

Mr. Spirodes was a tall man, well-muscled, his broad shoulders topped by a magnificent head with graying black hair. His wife was short and plump; her lustrous dark eyes shone with pleasure as she greeted her guests.

"Welcome, welcome, Jim!" she said, holding out her hands. "It's been too long since we've seen you! And these are your children?"

"Two of them are, Sophia," Jim Daring replied warmly. He introduced Mark and Penny, and then David. "David Curtis is a good friend of ours, visiting us from the States."

"All of you are most welcome," Mrs. Spirodes said.

Alexander had already paid the taxi driver when Jim Daring turned to do that. "Here, Alex, let me do that," he'd said, but too late.

Two men had come and taken their bags from the cab, and before the travelers knew it, they had been shown to their rooms in the guest wing of the house. Penny had a room, her father another, and the boys shared a third.

Penny marveled at the high-ceilinged room, the long windows, the marvelous pale green drapes and carpets. "This is wonderful, Mrs. Spirodes!" she exclaimed.

Mark and David stood gazing at the models of ancient Greek ships. Intricately crafted wooden models in glass cases adorned the hallway and a marvelously constructed model ship decorated the dresser in their room. They couldn't wait to ask Mr. Spirodes about these ancient fighting vessels with their banks of oars, their sails, and the battering rams that protruded from the bows.

Soon the Darings gathered back in the large study of the home, drinking fragrant tea with their hosts.

"My latest project has been constructing a real galley, Jim!" Mr. Spirodes said, his large face beaming. "We've built it precisely according to the ancient design, absolutely authentic in every detail—except for some modern equipment which we've added," he said, his eyes twinkling.

He sat on a long sea-green sofa, with his wife beside him. On the wall behind them was a large painting of a galley under full sail. The banks of oars extending from either side looked so real that it seemed about to plunge from the canvas into the room. Mark and David couldn't take their eyes off the picture!

Mr. Spirodes laughed at their openmouthed admiration of the painting. "That's the picture that gave me the idea," he said. "It's an Athenian trireme, a warship with three banks of oars. I've loved that picture for years, and for years I've sat at my desk across the room, staring at it, wishing I could transport myself back into time and sail on it. How I longed to do that!"

He shook his large head, looking himself like a statue of an ancient Greek god, David thought. Mr. Spirodes sipped his tea, then continued.

"One day, two years ago, I suddenly thought to myself, *If I can't go back in time to sail that boat, why not bring it to me? Why not build it?* From that day, I couldn't get the idea out of my head. It just wouldn't go away."

He jumped up and began to pace the room. "I'm a sailor, as you know, Jim. I've sailed the Mediterranean for years, and into the Atlantic as well. I know boats. And this idea kept banging around in my head! I couldn't get rid of it!"

Mr. Spirodes stood and looked again at the painting on the wall. The eyes of everyone in the room followed his.

How real it looked! David could picture the man on the quarterdeck of such a galley, clad in armor, directing his fighting ship to ram an enemy vessel!

"So I brought my father here one evening, and put the matter to him," Mr. Spirodes continued. "Since my mother died, he's really had nothing to do that interested him. 'Dad,' I told him that night, after we'd eaten one of Sophia's magnificent dinners, 'look at that ship! You gave it to me when I married Sophia. I love it, but it's tormented me for years. And why? Because I can look at it, but I can't sail on it. That's why! Now, I've got an idea. Why don't you build it for me?'"

Mr. Spirodes threw back his magnificent head and laughed a booming laugh. "He was astounded, I can tell you that! He was simply astounded. And do you know, Jim, he knew I meant it. He knew I'd been trying to find something for him to work on. And he also knew I really wanted that boat. So he said he would."

He paused, standing before the sofa, looking at the great canvas with the blue water and white caps and the brown-hulled vessel with light sails coming right at him. No one said anything. Clearly, this was very important to him.

Then he came back to the present. "Can you believe it, Jim? Since then, my father's been a new man. For two years he's directed the building of this galley. We've worked on it together, of course, but he's done the lion's share. He's the real builder, the real director of the project.

Of course we had to make some modern adaptations." His dark eyes gleamed with pleasure as he spoke; his whole body was animated. "We can't possibly pay for a crew of 200 men, including 170 oarsmen to row the thing! So we put in diesel engines. We've made places for one bank of oars in the hull. And, naturally, we put in radio and radar to warn of approaching ships. And we've got the latest navigational equipment."

Mr. Spirodes strode back and forth across the room, almost forgetting his guests were there, telling of the things they'd done to the boat. "We put in some storage space where the rowers would have been. We have a nice lounge and kitchen, and we made cabins in the hull below the deck— some modern cabins, Jim—with a couple of showers in the hall! We plan to take groups of friends and historians on tours to the sites of ancient Greek history and mythology. Already museums have asked to borrow the ship for their own cruises. And three movie companies want to use it in their films."

He threw back his head and laughed his booming laugh again. "I think we've started a trend. The local museum has sponsored an official model kit and it's selling like crazy! Everyone's interested in ancient galleys now."

"How big is the ship, Mr. Spirodes?" David asked eagerly.

"One hundred feet long, David. Many of the ancient triremes were longer than that, but we thought that was a good size for our purposes. It's nineteen feet wide. Those ships were slim, built for speed and easy steering. They were designed to spin like a top when the oarsmen on one side pulled and those on the opposite side pushed. Then their aim was to drive their ram into the side of an enemy ship. One clear blow with that ram, and the other ship had a hole that soon let the ocean in!"

He stopped and looked at the painting again. "Curiously, the ships didn't sink! They were made of light wood, many of silver ash, like ours. When their sides were rammed, they'd fill with water, and their men would be out of action, helpless in the ocean. The fleet that was victorious would tow the damaged enemy vessels to shore and repair them."

"When can we see the galley?" Daring asked eagerly.

"Tomorrow morning!" Mr. Spirodes beamed. "Then you and I can finish our business in the afternoon, Jim. My lawyer tells me the papers your people sent are all in proper order. Just explain the matter to me, and show me where to sign!"

"I'll certainly do that, Alex!" Daring said with a laugh.

The youngsters were thrilled. Would they be able to go on board the vessel?

Mr. Spirodes answered the question in their minds before they could even ask.

"In fact," Mr. Spirodes said, "how would you like to take a cruise?" He looked at the teenagers.

"We'd love to do that, sir!" Mark answered for the three of them.

"All right, we'll go down to the port in the morning, look the boat over, then take a ride in the harbor."

David and Mark were so excited that they thought they'd never get to sleep that night. It took about four minutes. Jim Daring and Alex talked long into the night.

CHAPTER 3

A FIGHTING GALLEY

I don't want you to see it from the dock," Mr. Spirodes said. "I want you to see it from water level first." He'd parked the car, then led them to a small motorboat tied to the wharf. Jim Daring and the teenagers followed him down the steps to the landing.

They got into the blue craft and Mr. Spirodes started the engine. "Bring in those lines, boys," he told them. Mark and David lifted the looped lines from the hooks on the deck and threw them into the motorboat. Mr. Spirodes put the engine in gear, and the vessel picked up speed as they left the wharf and headed into the harbor.

Ships of all sizes, from all over the world, moved in the harbor or were tied at the various docks. Among the huge merchant ships were occasional warships of various navies. Mark, Penny, and David were anxious to see the galley, and Mark asked where it was, but Mr. Spirodes wouldn't tell them.

"It's so small when you compare it with the big ships in the harbor," he said, his eyes twinkling, "but it's majestic when you look up at it from water level. I want you to see it as a sailor from a disabled boat would have long ago, as

13

he clung to his oar and wondered who'd pick him up—his friends or the enemy!"

The blue sky had not a cloud. Harbor birds circled overhead, calling to each other, looking for fish and for the scraps that were thrown from the ships and boats. The small motorboat was moving quickly now, heading around a dock that stuck out from the land. Warehouses and sheds lined the shore beyond the docks.

Suddenly Mr. Spirodes pointed. "Look at that catamaran!"

His passengers followed his arm and looked to their right. There, swooping toward them, was a magnificent twin-hulled sailing boat. The two black hulls were connected by a deck between them, and the large sail rose from this platform. The sail was full; the craft was moving with great speed.

"Those are amazing boats," Mr. Spirodes said admiringly. "They were invented by the Pacific islanders centuries ago. People crossed the Pacific in those things, and colonized islands thousands of miles apart!"

"Why do they have two hulls?" Mark asked.

"For speed, and for stability," Mr. Spirodes replied. "Two hulls don't sit as deeply in the water as one would. They just skim across the surface. That boat is very much like your America's Cup winner—it'll go at least 20 knots!"

Mr. Spirodes squinted in the sunlight, looking more closely at the approaching craft. "They've really put the equipment on that one. Look at their radio antennae and their lights. They've even got radar!"

"How big is it, Mr. Spirodes?" David asked.

"I'd say it measures 50 feet, maybe a little longer. It can

carry a lot of people. They use these things all over the world for tour boats. Believe it or not, they've got cabins and bathrooms in those hulls. You'd be amazed at what they can carry. And to think that we Europeans didn't invent them!" He shook his head in wonder.

"That boat would catch us in short order," he commented. "In a favorable wind it can actually go a knot faster than the breeze itself."

Penny had a funny feeling as she looked at the black-hulled craft with its black sail. She'd aimed her camera at it, looking through the telephoto lens, and was surprised to see several men on the catamaran staring directly at them through binoculars. *Why would they be looking at us?* she wondered to herself.

"But look at what we Europeans *did* invent!" Mr. Spirodes continued. He'd steered the boat around a wharf and turned toward shore. There before them was the galley!

Then Penny realized that those men on the catamaran might be looking at the galley, not at Mr. Spirodes' motorboat. But she still felt strange about the black craft, and she wasn't sure why. Finally she turned her head in the direction Mr. Spirodes pointed.

All of them were stunned at the sight. The graceful warship from ancient times loomed before them as the motorboat drew close. Two masts towered above them, the tall one amidships, and a shorter one forward. Heading toward the bow of the ship, they saw the curved hull slope back and down, then curve forward as it met the water.

Now Penny could see that the shorter mast near the bow

of the boat leaned forward. The ship was light brown in color, although there was a black stripe just above the waterline.

"Why is the galley painted black along the waterline?" she asked.

"They painted the hulls of warships with pine tar and pitch to protect them from the sea worms that ate the wood, Penny. Merchant ships were sheathed in lead, but warships needed speed, and the lead would have slowed them down. So they used tar and pitch."

"How big are the sails, Mr. Spirodes?" Mark asked.

"The mainsail's about 250 square feet, Mark," Mr. Spirodes replied. "The foresail is one-fourth that size. You'll see when we get on board that the man at the steering wheel can also drop the mainsail if he sees danger ahead or a strong wind coming. Usually, other men take care of that while he steers."

"Look at the ram!" Mr. Spirodes pointed to the sloping bow that curved back toward the water level. "The point's just under the water. One good blow and that giant ram would crush a hole in the side of the foe. That's all it took; they had no compartments to speak of. One strike with the ram, and the enemy was out of the fight with its men helpless in the water."

"Where are the oars, Mr. Spirodes?" Mark asked as they drew close and the side of the ship loomed above them.

"They're on shore, Mark," he replied. "It takes a lot of men to row a boat this size, as I explained, and we're only going to use oars on special occasions. Most of the time we'll use the sails. Except when we're in a hurry—then we'll use the diesels." He grinned at Daring. "That's one of the concessions we've made to modern times. Another is the radio and radar equipment. With so many boats sailing the seas these days, we've got to have that kind of equipment for safety's sake. But we keep it as hidden as we can."

Then they were at the side of the ship. Mr. Spirodes cut the engine, and told the boys to tie the bow and stern with the lines hanging beside the stepladder that rose along the galley's side. He led them up this ladder to the deck above.

"Welcome aboard, Captain," a hearty voice boomed as Mr. Spirodes stepped onto the deck of the ship. Mr. Daring and the kids followed, and were introduced to a man as big as Mr. Spirodes himself. "This is Carlos Mercuri, the mate," Mr. Spirodes said.

A tall, powerfully built man in white shirt and trousers, his large head crowned with black thick hair, Carlos strode forward with a welcoming smile. He shook hands with Alex, and was then introduced to Daring and the teenagers.

The boys felt the strength in his hand, and at once they liked the friendly, open-faced sailor. He welcomed them all at great length and offered to show them the ship.

"Take them around, Carlos," Alex said, "while I call the office." He went to the cabin in the stern, stepped down a few steps, and disappeared.

Carlos, beaming with pride, led them around the reconstructed galley. First he went forward along the central open passage, pointing to the places where rowers would have sat in ancient times.

"We've even put canopies over the rowers," he said,

"which protected them from volleys of arrows when the ship was in battle. These canopies ran along each side of the deck, shielding the rowers below them. But notice! Where they had rowers, we've put in cabins, small but very comfortable cabins. Many groups have already asked to rent this boat for trips and excursions."

Carlos's English was laced with a thick accent, and Penny was intrigued. "Where did you learn to speak English, Mr. Carlos?" she asked curiously.

"In England, Penny," he answered. "My brother took me with him to England one winter. What a terrible climate! And I learned there."

"Is he a sailor, too?" Mark asked.

Carlos laughed. "No, indeed, Mark! He's an inside man. He works in museums. That would kill me, being cooped up inside a building all my life. But he loves it!" The three teenagers looked at the powerful man and realized he was right. He'd be like a caged bird if he were confined to a museum or an office. Carlos laughed again at the thought of spending his life as his brother did.

But Penny was puzzled at Carlos's answer. She knew lots of people from England, and she knew others who'd learned English there; but his accent was different from any she'd ever heard.

Carlos strode vigorously before them until they reached the foredeck, which was raised above the main deck by several feet. "Here's where archers and soldiers would take their positions for battle," he explained. "They'd fire arrows at the soldiers and steersmen in the enemy galleys, and then be ready to fight with spears and swords if an enemy ship came alongside."

Next they followed him to the high curved post at the very front of the ship. Here Carlos leaned over and pointed down to the deadly ram below. "That was the main weapon of these warships. That's what they tried to slam into the side of enemy ships. One blow from that ram, and their victim ship filled with water and settled until the decks were awash. They'd float, but they couldn't be rowed. They were helpless, out of action completely, just waiting to be picked up and towed to shore by the victors."

Daring and the three teens looked over the bow. There, curving into the water from the hull, was the deadly ram. Its menacing end was just below the surface of the water.

"Why isn't the point sharper?" Daring asked Carlos.

"No need. The force of a moving ship behind that blunt tip smashed the wooden hull of anything it struck. They wanted to make as big a hole as they could, so they made it blunt, with three projections which were sheathed in bronze."

Carlos continued "And they had another problem. If they hit a ship at the wrong angle, the motion of their target could tear the ram off their own boat. So the rams were made to disengage if that happened. The weight of the ram's bronze sheathing was offset by the bulk of the light wood inside. A loose ram wouldn't sink too deeply in the water. The rams were expensive and sailors always tried to recover them."

Daring and the teens were fascinated as Carlos told of ancient sea fights, of strategy and tactics. Then he led them back to the stern of the ship.

Several sailors were working at various tasks along the deck, and Carlos introduced these men as they passed. "They're all Greeks," he explained. "Several of them were recruited by Alex and his father. It's a good crew."

"What are they doing?" Penny asked.

"They are making the ship ready for a voyage," he replied. "We're going on a long voyage tomorrow."

"Where will you go?" Mark asked eagerly.

"To the famous island of Rhodes. That's east of Greece and south of Istanbul," Carlos replied. "The officials there are planning a civic celebration of an ancient local holiday, and they've asked us to visit and let people see a real galley. Rhodes is the fourth largest of Greece's many islands. That's where the Knights of St. John made their headquarters during the Crusades. They built strongholds there, and guarded the routes of pilgrims to the Holy Land."

"How long a voyage is that, Mr. Mercuri?" David asked, intrigued.

"Oh, not quite 300 miles the way we're going. We'll make a couple of stops at small islands along the way. During the daytime we'll use our sails for a few hours, if the winds are favorable. Mostly, though, we'll use the engines. We're testing all our equipment on this trip."

He took them below and showed them the captain's cabin in the stern. Then he led them along the narrow passage against the left side of the hull, and pointed to the cabins on the right.

"We've arranged the cabins as the Greeks arranged their

ships for carrying cavalry and their horses," he explained. "They'd have half the horses along one side of the ship, say from the bow to midships, with a passageway opposite the horse stalls. Then, at midships, the passageway would veer to the other side of the ship, and the horse stalls from there to the stern would be on the opposite side of the ship. That way the weight would be evenly distributed."

They came to the end of the passage toward the bow and stopped before a narrow door. "Here's the storage space," Carlos said. Opening the door he led them into a rather spacious compartment. He pointed to the ringbolts along the deck and set in the bulkheads. "Those are walls to you people," he laughed. "On shipboard, walls are 'bulkheads,' floors are 'decks,' and ropes are 'lines.' "

There were two rows of barrels in the forward part of this compartment, David noticed. A dozen barrels sat on each side, in two rows. Each barrel was tied to ringbolts set in the deck.

"What's in those barrels?" David asked.

"Supplies of all kinds," Carlos replied. "We've tried to do it the old-fashioned way. We've also got ship's stores, extra gear, and fuel for the diesel engines. We've made special barrels for that so we won't have to use the modern drums and spoil the looks!" He laughed. "We've really combined ancient and modern things for the most effective job, but we want it to look as authentic as possible."

Carlos fell silent then, and looked at the line of barrels on the right side for a long moment. There were twelve of them, in two rows of six each, with red ropes around the tops.

Carlos smiled as he continued. "We took in the last of our stores last night, in fact. We're ready for sea now. Those twelve barrels in front on the left hold bricks for ballast. The rest hold our supplies." He looked again at the barrels on the right. Then he laughed, but didn't explain why. Penny wondered what he was thinking.

"Let's go!" he said suddenly, as he turned toward the steps at the front end of the compartment. They followed him to the open deck above. Walking toward the stern, they saw Alex Spirodes waiting for them up on the quarterdeck by the wheel.

"What do you think of our galley?" he called.

"It's fabulous, Alex!" Daring replied. "What a marvelous thing you and your dad have done!"

Alex's great laugh made them laugh in return. The man had such pleasure in this ship! "Let's show our guests how she handles, Carlos," Alex said.

"Aye, aye, Captain," the big man replied with a laugh. He called the crew to their stations and the boat made ready to sail.

"Did Carlos tell you that with our two engines we can spin this ship like lightning—just as they did in ancient times—and use our ram if we have to?"

"No, he didn't," Jim Daring replied.

Mr. Spirodes laughed his booming laugh. "I've even reinforced the bow so that we really could ram another ship," he said. "No sense having the thing if you can't use it!"

The teenagers were to remember these words.

CHAPTER 4

READY FOR SEA

We'll use the diesels for this run," Alex explained, as Daring and the youngsters climbed the steps to the quarterdeck. "But tomorrow we'll raise the sails and see how she handles with those. Did Carlos tell you that we're going to Rhodes?"

"He did indeed, Alex," Daring replied, "and the kids here started looking for places where they could stow away for the ride! In fact, they saw some likely looking barrels below, and said they might jump in those!"

Alex laughed again; then he grew suddenly serious. "Why not, Jim?" he asked. "We could take them with us for a couple of days, at least." He saw the faces of the three light up at the prospect and warmed to the new idea. "In fact, we'll get them back to Athens by Friday. Dad won't be able to sail with us tomorrow. He's going to fly out by seaplane and meet us at Rhodes. I'll be coming back on that plane, and the kids could fly back with me."

Mark, Penny, and David could hardly believe their ears. Sail on a real Greek galley through the Mediterranean to the historic island of Rhodes! They were beside themselves.

"How about it, Jim? I'd love to have them! You could come yourself if you didn't have other work in Athens."

Mr. Daring stood in thought, pondering the idea, and Alex pressed the case. "Are you going to make these fine young people wait around with nothing to do while you poke through contracts and meet boring businessmen in Athens?"

The three teens knew better than to badger Mr. Daring while he thought about it. But, of course, he loved the idea of their having this trip in the Mediterranean with his trusted friend as much as they did.

"Trying to make me feel guilty, are you, Alex?" Daring laughed. "I can't go, much as I'd like to. But if they'd like the trip, it's fine with me."

"Dad, we'd love to!" Penny exclaimed, and the boys added their enthusiastic agreement.

Daring laughed at their eagerness and excitement. "Looks like you've got a deal, Alex," he said. "This is very generous of you. Sure they won't be in the way?"

"Nonsense, Jim. We'll put them to work at once. The boys are strong. We'll have them hauling sails and learning how to steer this ship. Maybe we'll let them bail out the bilge with buckets! And Penny will have incredible opportunities to take pictures. We'll pass all kinds of ships and boats. She'll see dolphins and birds that she's never seen before. It'll be a real adventure for them, Jim." Alex was clearly pleased at the prospect of having them with him.

"Take them along, then, with my thanks. I'll be in Athens three more days in any case," he said, laughing at the tremendous pleasure in the faces of Mark, Penny, and David. "I'll keep myself busy somehow. Just be sure to bring them back with you. Their mothers would never forgive me if they stowed away on your galley for the summer!"

"I promise, Jim. I'll bring them back on the plane with me Friday. They'll have Tuesday, Wednesday, and Thursday on the ship with me. That should give them a taste of ancient sailing! We'll be back in Athens for lunch Friday." He beamed at the three, and they beamed back in high excitement.

Mark, Penny, and David looked at each other and tried not to laugh. Who would have thought that they'd have such an adventure? And they'd never flown on a seaplane before. Imagine landing and taking off on the water! They could hardly contain themselves.

By then the ship had become very busy. The crew was casting off lines, the engines were purring smoothly, and Alex Spirodes was ready to steer the ancient galley away from the dock and out into the harbor. They'd have a trial cruise for a couple of hours, he told them, and a real sea voyage tomorrow!

"This will be a good test for you," Mr. Spirodes laughed. "If you get seasick, you don't have to go with us tomorrow!" He threw back his head and laughed his booming laugh.

They didn't get sick. They loved it!

That night, after dinner at the Mr. Spirodes, they packed their things for the voyage. "Wear pants or your divided skirt, Penny," Daring told his daughter. "They'll be the most comfortable—and modest—clothes for climbing around a boat."

"Take a couple of sweaters, too," Sophia Spirodes advised them. "It gets cool on the water at night and sometimes during the day. Do you have jackets?"

"Yes, we do, Mrs. Spirodes," Penny replied.

"Fine," their hostess said. "Remember that we have more if you need them."

They packed clothes for their three-day trip, while Alex Spirodes told them of seafaring in ancient times. They were gathered in Mr. Daring's room, packing their clothes in the one bag each would take on the voyage.

Suddenly, Sophia Spirodes rushed back into the room. "Alex, Jim, come quickly! There's terrible news on the television!"

They all rushed out of the room and into the small den. There a television newscaster was replaying the transfer of the art treasures from the Archaeological Museum to the van that would take them to the ship for transfer to London. The reporter was speaking in Greek, of course, which the Americans couldn't understand.

But they could understand the importance of the event. They gasped as special photos of the ancient art pieces were flashed on the screen. They saw the assistant director, Andropous Lycenus, and were impressed with the man's magnificent bearing.

What a profile he has! Penny thought to herself, as the orator turned his head and she caught a full view of his photogenic features. He looked like statues of ancient Greek heroes she'd seen in books.

Again the television showed the events of the previous

day. Standing around the television set, they saw the white van with police motorcycles and squad cars before and behind it as the procession left the museum and headed through Athens for the seaport 18 miles away. They saw the barrels unloaded at the docks and put on board ship under the heaviest security. Armed guards were everywhere.

"The security arrangements were incredible," Mr. Spirodes translated for the Americans. "The art is being loaned to the British Museum in London, and will be displayed there for four months. Andropous Lycenus is the assistant director of the museum. He's better known to the public than the director, in fact, because he's often in the news."

Then the crime was announced. The barrels from the museum had been inspected on shipboard before the ship sailed for London. The Greek treasures were not in them! The dozen barrels were filled with bricks instead!

"The nation's in an uproar," Alex translated, his face stricken with the shock. "This is a cultural catastrophe! Those things are irreplaceable! Absolutely irreplaceable!" He shook his head in sadness.

Next the television showed interviews with the museum director in Sweden, the distinguished and honored Demetrius Polodorus. The poor man was in tears. He'd turned the whole business over to his outstanding assistant, Andropous Lycenus—who was also missing!

The announcer then interviewed the head of the company responsible for transferring the ancient treasures. This man gave an elaborate description of the complex security precautions his company had taken. Never had they failed to deliver a shipment of value. He too was in shock.

Mr. Spirodes translated the interviews with police and government officials. "They inspected the barrels before they were brought out to the van," he said. "They certified that they contained the art. The security company's guards then went to the van and took their places inside. They rode to the ship with the barrels and never let them out of their sight. The shipment went into a special storage compartment on the ship, and the guards watched this in shifts."

He stopped translating and listened to the latest speculation. "They're now saying that the only time the barrels were not guarded by the security company was after they were sealed in the museum. That's when the barrels were left in the care of the museum guards, while the security guards took their places in the van."

"That's it, Sophia," Alex exclaimed suddenly, pounding his knee with his huge fist. "That's it! There had to be a switch between the time the barrels were sealed and when they were brought out to the van. That's the only time it could have been done."

"That's what the police say," she answered. "They also say that Andropous Lycenus's disappearance is a mystery. There's no clue to where he might be. Nor can they find the two museum guards who watched the barrels when the security company men were going to the van."

"Does Lycenus have any family?" Daring asked.

"Not anymore," Sophia answered. "His parents and his one brother are no longer alive. His wife died three years ago, and they had no children."

"What do they think happened to him?" Penny asked, shocked at this tragedy to Lycenus, to the museum, and to Greece.

"They don't know," Sophia replied. "They simply don't know." She dabbed her eyes with her handkerchief. "Oh this is awful!"

"The museum's in an uproar," Alex said. "Rather, all Greece is in an uproar! The entire museum staff is being questioned. No one else is missing but Lycenus and the two guards."

"Hush, Alex!" Sophia said suddenly. "They're talking about Lycenus again."

They were all silent as Alex and Sophia hung on the words of the latest news. A picture of a battered white sports car flashed on the screen. The car was being dragged from the water at the bottom of a steep cliff. A narrow highway curved sharply around the hill above.

"That car belongs to Andropous Lycenus," Alex translated. "They're saying he missed a turn. He loves to race that car, they say, and must have been going too fast. He didn't make the turn. The car went off the cliff and into the sea. They haven't found his body."

"The police suspect murder," Sophia added, as the newscaster interviewed a uniformed officer at the site of the wreck. "They say he was a fast driver, but he knew his car and he knew this road. The officer is saying he would not have missed the turn. It's on the way to his home, and he went around that curve every day."

The news ended then. Alex sadly turned off the set.

"They're closing down the nation! They'll search every merchant and passenger ship, every train, every truck, every car that leaves Greece. The police believe that the barrels with the art treasures have been taken to a secure hiding place, and that the thieves won't dare try to move the treasures out of Greece for a year at least. They'll lie low, wait for the security to loosen—it'll have to—and then move them out."

"But who would buy those treasures?" Sophia asked. "Everyone will know they're stolen. The thieves will never be able to sell them."

"On the contrary, Sophia," her husband replied. "Well-known art is stolen all the time. There are rich people all around the world who buy such treasure through the black market and hide it in their private homes. No one, but they, ever sees it again."

He continued, "This art will sell for millions, and make someone very rich indeed."

"But it robs Greece, doesn't it?" Daring asked.

"It does, Jim," Mr. Spirodes said heavily. "It does."

They were all depressed by this blow to Greek culture and history.

Mark, Penny, and David went back to Daring's room and completed their packing. Daring came in after a while. "Let's read the Bible before we turn in." He opened to the book they'd been studying this week—Esther. They took turns reading how God miraculously delivered the Jews from the malice of their enemies. Then they prayed.

After a night's sleep, they would be ready for tomorrow's voyage!

CHAPTER 5

THE SEAS OF ULYSSES

These are the seas in the legend of Ulysses!" David announced, as the three stood at the bow of the galley and felt the salt spray that struck the prow below them. The ship had left Athens nine hours ago, at 7A.M., in fact, and the diesel engines had driven them steadily south through the Adriatic Sea.

As soon as they'd come aboard early that morning, Alex Spirodes had gone into the cabin and called the harbor-master, who was an old friend. "Stephanos, I heard the awful news about the theft of our treasures. As you know, I'm taking the galley to Rhodes today. The news reports say every ship and car and plane is being searched for the lost art. When can you come look us over and give us clearance?"

"Thanks for calling, Alex. Actually, your mate, Carlos, telephoned me last night and suggested the same thing. I told him we knew you too well to bother with searching your ship, but he insisted. I came down this morning about six o'clock and inspected your cargo. Just stores, as Carlos had told me. You're clear; you can sail any time you wish."

And so they had. By prearrangement, large numbers of newspeople and TV cameras covered their departure from port. The galley had aroused national interest, and the networks not only of Greece but of other European nations were there. Watched by millions, the marvelous ship set sail and glided gracefully to sea.

Ashore, the TV reporters repeated the previous night's story about the tragic theft of ancient art. They told how the nation had been locked tight by security forces. The military had joined the nation's police in guarding every border, checking every car, ship, plane, and train that left the country.

So far, nothing had been found. No clue to the missing men had been discovered. No hint of the treasures' whereabouts had been discerned.

While the country was sealed tight, the graceful ship sailed the Aegean Sea of Ulysses, heading south. Narrators on the various European networks described ancient war galleys, told of the building of this ship, and replayed interviews with Alex and his father as they described their love for ancient Greek vessels and their construction of this replica. For millions of viewers, their nation's history came alive as the warship from times gone by sailed before their eyes.

Once clear of Greece, Alex Spirodes turned the vessel east. In the middle of the afternoon, however, he stopped the engines and unfurled the two sails. The ship's speed had been cut in half, but Mark and Penny and David agreed that the sensation of actually sailing an ancient galley more than made up for it.

Choppy seas caused the ship to pitch and roll as it plowed its way steadily eastward toward the island of Rhodes. White spray splashed back from the bow of the ship and its blunt ram. Above them, half the sky was clear blue; the rest was spotted with bright cumulus clouds. Seabirds periodically came soaring by, looking for scraps of food from the ship.

"The apostles Paul, Timothy and Luke, sailed these seas almost 2000 years ago!" David said.

David and Penny stood at the bow, holding to the taut lines that rose from the deck to the masts above and behind them. Mark, however, was showing off his "sea legs," he claimed, by balancing on widespread feet with his hands on his hips.

"You'd better hold on to the line, Mark!" his sister warned. "The waves are getting bigger."

Mark laughed. "Only wimps and girls hold on to lines. Real sailors know how to balance."

"Mark!" Penny warned again.

Her brother threw back his head and laughed confidently. Feet spread wide, arms akimbo, he looked, she thought, like a modern buccaneer, with his powerful frame clothed in khaki shorts and blue polo shirt.

"I guess I can handle waves," he reminded her.

The ship shuddered suddenly as a large wave hit with unexpected force. Mark plunged forward, and would have fallen face first into the wooden rail if David's powerful hand hadn't grabbed his arm and checked his fall. Mark collapsed to his knees on the deck, his face barely missing the rail.

"Mark!" Penny cried in alarm.

The ship's deck fell and rose again, and Mark got slowly to his feet, rubbing a bruised knee. His face wore a sheepish grin as he turned to David and said, "Thanks!"

"No problem," David replied. "Just glad I can help a real sailor sometimes!" he said with a perfectly straight face.

Penny laughed at Mark's expression as he took in David's words. David laughed, too, as he looked at her. She wore khaki slacks, a white blouse, and white tennis shoes. Her hair was pulled back in a ponytail held by a white bow. *Wow, she's pretty!* he thought—for the thousandth time in the last four weeks.

Her eyes sparkled at David. "Do you think we'll ever be real sailors, David? I mean *real sailors* like Mark?"

"Not a chance, Penny," he said solemnly. "Girls and wimps hold on to lines. *Real* sailors balance without holding on to anything. We'll never be that good—not like Mark."

"But look at Carlos and Mr. Spirodes and the other men," she protested, with a straight face. "They hold on sometimes when the seas are rough. Aren't they real sailors?" Her pretty face appeared confused.

"Not really," David answered with a serious expression. "They're good but not great. Real sailors are great. That's why they never have to hold on."

"O.K., O.K., cut it out!" Mark said. "I admit it. That wave caught me by surprise."

"Well," David continued, "what I was saying before Mark's acrobatics interrupted me, was that these are the legendary Seas of Ulysses. We're sailing in historic waters! He sailed this way over 3,000 years ago."

"Where was he going?" Mark asked, testing David's knowledge of Homer's ancient mythical hero.

"Home. He was going home. That is, he was *trying* to go home."

"What stopped him?" Mark asked.

"Poseidon, the Greek god of the ocean. That's who stopped him. He was mad at Ulysses for blinding his giant son, so he caused storms and all kinds of troubles to keep Ulysses from reaching home for ten years! He was trying to kill him, but the goddess Athena protected Ulysses."

The boys discussed the ancient Greek legends that the poet Homer had immortalized in his two great works, *The Iliad* and *The Odyssey*. David had read both; Mark was reading *The Iliad.*

"I'm getting bogged down in these endless battles," Mark said. "Maybe I should skip the rest and start *The Odyssey.*"

"Better not," David advised. "*The Iliad* is one of the world's great books, and you should finish it. That's where you learn what the ancient Greeks really thought about their gods. They had a horribly confused view of reality, and it comes out in Homer's story. *The Iliad* tells how the Greeks tried to capture the city of Troy for 10 years, but failed because they couldn't storm its tall walls."

"How'd they win, then?" Penny asked.

"Ulysses," David replied. "He was the shrewd one, the master of planning and stratagem. He came up with a brilliant plan."

"What was it?" she asked.

" 'Let's build a huge wooden horse,' he said. 'We'll roll

it on wheels to the city gate, and then sail away. They'll think we're giving up, and are leaving a sacrifice to the gods.' "

"How would that help the Greeks take the city?" Mark asked skeptically. Actually, he knew the story, even though he hadn't read the book.

" 'Put men in the wooden horse,' Ulysses told them. 'At night, they can sneak out, rush the gate, and open it for our army. We'll sail back in the darkness and position ourselves outside. Once the gate's open, we'll rush in and take the city while most of their men are still asleep!' "

David continued, "And that's what they did! That's how they captured Troy. But when the Greeks sailed home with all their prisoners and loot, they ran into trouble. And that's when Ulysses angered Poseidon, god of the sea. He made Ulysses sail for 10 years before he could get home. Then. . . "

"Penny!" An excited shout from Alex Spirodes interrupted David's tale. Turning, they looked back toward the stern, where Alex stood with Carlos and the big blond crewman who'd joined the ship the night before. Alex pointed over the right side of the ship. "Get your camera!"

The three jammed the rail and looked down. Dolphins! A school of dolphins had come up beside the ship. Five or six of the creatures were sporting close beside the galley, cruising with easy grace, rising to the surface, then curving back into the blue water. Never had Mark, Penny, or David been so close to the lovely animals.

With a cry of delight Penny stooped to the deck and took her camera from its case. She aimed and focused quickly, taking picture after picture. The dolphins' sleek gray bodies glistened in the bright sunlight and clear water near the surface.

The boys were spellbound, as were the other men on the ship who were lining the rail to watch the creatures below.

"Look how they love an audience!" Penny exclaimed between shots. "They're laughing!"

"With us or at us?" David asked.

"With us," she said. "They're laughing with us. They know we love to watch them swim, and they love to give us a show."

"Get that one, Penny!" Mark said suddenly, pointing back to the stern. "He's almost touching the ship!"

Turning quickly, Penny focused with practiced ease and took several pictures of a the dolphin that swam so close. Twisting the zoom lens to adjust for the distance, she brought the dolphin's face so near she felt she could reach out and touch it!

Then she raised her camera a bit, and focused on Carlos and the new sailor as they gazed down at the dolphin. Alex must have gone below. *This will be a fine shot!* she thought to herself. She snapped twice, then paused to look at the new man who seemed so close in the telephoto lens. They'd not seen him the day before. Carlos had said that the man had joined them at the last minute, replacing a crewman who'd had to stay ashore.

The man was tall, broad-shouldered, well-muscled, with thick blond hair and an eyepatch over his left eye.

"He looks like a real pirate," Mark had said that morning

after meeting the new man. "Give him a cutlass and a brace of pistols, and he'd be the perfect buccaneer!"

Penny had been struck earlier by the man's resemblance to Carlos, the ship's mate. Now she studied his face through the powerful zoom lens. He laughed at something Carlos said and turned to the side so that she could see his profile.

What a magnificent head! she thought to herself. *I've got to get his picture.* He was really a striking figure, and she took several shots as the man talked.

Then something exploded in Penny's mind! She had seen that magnificent head and profile before—and recently. But not with blond hair. And not with an eye patch. But where? And when?

Thoughts tumbled confusedly in her head as she struggled to recall the answers to her questions. *Forget the blond hair,* she said to herself. *And forget the eyepatch, too. Just think of that head and profile. Where have I seen him?*

She took two more pictures. Then she remembered! The television report from the Archaeological Museum! The shipment of ancient Greek art to London! The magnificently photogenic assistant director, Andropous Lycenus, eloquent before the reporters as he described the loan of art to the British Museum!

The missing assistant director—I've found him! she thought suddenly to herself. She was sure of it.

Then the man turned and looked straight at her. He was 100 feet away actually, but the zoom lens made him seem just inches from her face. For a moment she didn't notice as she wrestled with the awful thought that she had found the man responsible for the robbery of Greek antiquities. Then she realized she'd been looking directly into his eyes for a long moment!

CHAPTER 6

ANDROPOUS LYCENUS

Quickly she turned her camera to the right, focused on another of the crew, and took his picture. Not daring to glance at the blond seaman to see if he was still watching her, she continued focusing on other sights, sweeping gradually around to her right until she felt she could put the camera down.

Turning back to the bow, she fumbled with the camera, covering the lens with its cap. Her face was pale; her heart was pounding.

"What's wrong, Penny?" David said anxiously, seeing the alarmed expression on her face. He reached out quickly and held her arm. Was she sick?

"Don't look back, David—or Mark. Keep looking around, as if nothing's happened. That blond sailor with the eye patch is Andropous Lycenus, the assistant director of the museum, the man who arranged the shipment of the Greek art to London!"

"But his car went into the sea!" Mark said, shocked by

40

her words. By an effort of will he kept his eyes on his sister, resisting the terrible temptation to look toward the stern.

"His car did—but he didn't! I'm sure that's who it is."

"But this man's got blond hair—we saw him this morning. The man on TV had black hair," David said.

"He didn't have an eye patch, either," Mark added. "Penny, what makes you so sure that this sailor is Lycenus?"

"His profile. I was struck by his profile when we saw the TV program. You know how I study faces. I really don't forget them—especially not someone as striking as that man. He looks like a statue of an ancient Greek hero!" *What did this mean—Lycenus, disguised as a sailor, on the galley?* Her heart was thudding.

Mark and David looked soberly at each other. Penny didn't often make mistakes about faces. She noticed everything, they'd learned, and she remembered what she saw.

"I saw him real close in the zoom lens," she continued. "I sure hope he didn't get suspicious." Had Lycenus noticed her long concentration on him? "There's another thing," Penny added. "I think Lycenus and Carlos are brothers!"

"What?" Mark asked, shocked. "Didn't the TV say that Lycenus's parents and brother were dead? Why do you say that, Penny?"

"Because when I saw them together in the zoom lens, the resemblance is really striking. They have the same build and the same type head. I think they have the same mannerisms, too."

"Then Lycenus wasn't murdered, as the police thought," David reasoned.

"Do you think he was behind the theft of the art?" Mark asked, his mind wrestling with the implications of this information. "Why else would he have disappeared?"

David suddenly grew alert. "Do you think the art is on this galley?"

"I don't see how it could be," Mark replied. "Carlos told Mr. Spirodes that he'd invited the police to search the ship this morning. Why would he do that if the art were here?"

"Maybe they knew it was hidden so well that it wouldn't be found," David answered.

"Maybe they knew that if they *asked* the police to inspect the ship, they wouldn't search too carefully!" Penny added. "Oh, this is awful!" Her brown eyes were troubled. "We've got to tell Mr. Spirodes," she said suddenly.

"You're right," Mark agreed.

Back at the stern of the ship, the blond man spoke quietly to Carlos. "Was that girl photographing us?"

"I don't think so," Carlos replied. "She takes pictures of everything and I think she was photographing the dolphins."

"I hope you're right," the blond man said soberly. He wasn't sure about this, but he accepted Carlos's explanation.

"But let's keep an eye on her," Carlos decided, turning and walking back to talk to the man at the wheel.

At the bow, the three wrestled with the awful implications of Penny's discovery. "How will we tell Mr. Spirodes?"she asked anxiously. "Carlos is always around. And will Mr. Spirodes believe me? After all, he trusts Carlos completely, and Carlos is the one who hired the blond man."

"We'll have to try," Mark said grimly. "At least he can be thinking about it. Maybe he'll want to search the ship himself, thoroughly, to make sure nothing's on board that shouldn't be."

"Could we look in the hold and see if anything's there that we didn't see yesterday?" David suggested. "I mean, before we tell Mr. Spirodes. If we found something that shouldn't be there, we'd have more to go on—and he'd have more reason to listen to us."

"We don't want those men to catch us snooping around," Penny said. "I think they're dangerous. And ruthless."

"I agree," David countered. "But we've got the run of the whole galley, Mr. Spirodes told us. I bet we could make an excuse. One of us could watch while the others searched the cargo." The more he thought of this, the more he liked the idea.

"That's a good idea, David!" Mark said. "Let's look for a chance to do that. Then we can tell him, and he can decide what he wants to do."

Gray clouds had covered the sky while they talked. The air grew colder. Penny shivered. "Think I'll get a sweater. Will one of you walk with me to my cabin?" She didn't want to be alone if she ran into Carlos or Lycenus.

"Sure," Mark answered. "David will go with you!" He grinned.

David's face grew red. Mark didn't often tease him about

his affection for Penny, and when he did, he always caught David by surprise. Penny made a face at her brother as she turned away, and Mark just grinned back at her.

David followed Penny down the steps to the deck, then to the nearest opening in the deck where more steps led to the passage below.

They were always surprised by the near-darkness of the passage after the brightness of the sky. Penny walked along the narrow red-paneled hallway, the cargo section to her right. Penny and David couldn't help glancing at the wall—the "bulkhead," Carlos had told them—as they passed, wondering what it contained that they hadn't seen the day before. Then they reached the middle of the ship, where the passage angled to their right so as to pass along the other side of the vessel. Now the cabins were on their left.

They walked to Penny's cabin, which was right next to the one Mark and David shared. Here she took out a sweater from the narrow closet. "Maybe I'm just nervous about the man we saw," she said in a low voice, as she pulled the sweater over her head.

"Well, the weather actually is colder," David reassured her. "Look out that port. The sky's getting darker all the time."

They both looked out the rectangular glassed port. The heavens were darker, Penny noticed. But she also knew that she was nervous.

"Can they hear us talking from the next cabin?" she asked.

"Mark and I tested that," David answered. "They can't.

And the cabin doors are insulated, too. These rooms were built to be quiet and restful. But we should still be careful. Let's go back on deck."

They left the cabin, turned right, and walked along the narrow passage. There were glassed ports on their left, through which they could see out. Then they came to the midsection. Here the passage veered to the right side of the ship. Now the ports were on that side. They mounted the stairs, walked to the foredeck, went up the steps, and rejoined Mark.

"Look at those ships!" he exclaimed, handing the binoculars to his sister. "It's an American carrier battle group! That's a huge aircraft carrier, a cruiser with incredible electronic weapons systems and dozens of missiles, a couple of destroyers, a supply ship, and two frigates. Boy, what power!"

Penny peered at the battle group. It was miles away, but the powerful binoculars made the gray warships seem very close. Then she handed the glasses to David, who looked eagerly at the deadly American task force.

"What carrier is that, David?" Mark asked.

"I think it's the *Nimitz*. My cousin, Carl, flies a Tomcat from that ship, and he told me he'd be in the Med this summer. There could be another battle group here, too, but I think that's the *Nimitz*."

"What are 'Tomcats'?" Penny asked.

"They're fighter planes," David answered. "Incredible fighter planes. They were built to protect the carrier battle groups against enemy aircraft, at very long range. They can carry the Phoenix missile—six of them, in fact—and

launch them at targets 140 miles away. Those planes can re-
fuel over and over again, and stay on patrol for hours in all
kinds of weather. They're equipped with radar so powerful
that they can detect enemy aircraft a long way away, and jam
enemy missiles coming after them. They're unbelievable aircraft. They're made by Grumman; Grumman has built navy
planes for decades."

The boys took turns watching the battle group through the
binoculars. *American ships!* Penny thought. *But they're so
far away—if only they could stay close to us!*

Mark stepped back from the wooden rail that lined the
ship and leaned casually against it as if he hadn't a care in
the world. Glancing at David, he resumed the discussion that
had been interrupted. "When should we look through that
cargo, David?"

"When we're sure the crew's not around." David stood
up and looked out to sea as he spoke. He pointed, and the
others looked at the large seabird that swooped toward the
ship, just skimming the surface. To watchers at the stern, the
three Americans appeared to be engrossed in nothing but the
sights around them.

"After they turn in for the night, then," Mark concluded.

"Did you see where the crewmen sleep?" Penny asked.

"In the front cabins," David said, "the ones nearest the
cargo hold."

"That means that we'll have to sneak past them to reach
the cargo hold," Mark said grimly.

"We've got to wait then," David said. "We'll have to
act as if nothing's wrong at supper."

He pulled out his paperback edition of Homer's *The Odyssey* and began to read about the voyages of Ulysses. Gradually, Penny and Mark became enthralled in the ancient tale, immersed in the plight of the wily Greek adventurer, lost in time as they heard the 3,000-year-old story.

That night at supper, Alex entertained the three Americans and Carlos with marvelous tales of adventures at sea. His tanned face beamed with pleasure as he answered their eager questions. He'd had amazing experiences over the course of an action-packed life, and he loved to tell his young friends about them.

But there was no opportunity for the three teens to speak to him in private!

CHAPTER 7

THE PLOT DISCLOSED

The three Americans came from below, walked along the deck, and proceeded to the foredeck just above the ram at the bow. The night sky was moonless. Clouds obscured the stars. Except for the running lights at bow and stern, midships, and on the two masts, the galley sailed in a sea of darkness and mystery.

The evening was cool and all three wore pants and sweaters. Penny stood between the two strong boys, leaning against the rail, gazing ahead into the darkness. David faced forward also, while Mark stood looking behind them so he could see anyone who might wander within earshot as they talked. Just below, waves splashed against the bow.

The ship was driven by its engines now, and the masts were bare. A crewman manned the wheel at the stern, glancing periodically at the radar screen that showed a large area of sea around the ship. The radar would warn them if other vessels came near during the night. This was an indispensable tool for modern navigation, one of the concessions Alexander Spirodes had made to technical progress.

At the bow of the ship, the three Americans could not hear the engines. The only sound was that of the prow cutting into the waves below and the wind whistling through the lines and the masts.

"I think the crew has turned in," Mark said.

"I do, too," David agreed. "Mr. Spirodes told Carlos he'd take the midnight watch, but Carlos said he'd already scheduled that for himself so Alex could get a rest."

"Where's Carlos now?" Penny asked. "And Lycenus?"

"In their cabin, I think," David replied. "I saw them both go in about half an hour ago."

"Do you think we could hear them talking?" she asked.

"Not from the hallway below," David said. "Mark and I tested that, and the rooms are almost soundproof."

"But what about through the port?" she asked. "Everyone's said how pleasant the weather is, and they might have left the port open. Could we stand on the deck above their cabin? Perhaps we can hear what they're saying. These are real criminals! We've got to find out what they might be planning to do to us."

"That's a great idea, Penny!" her brother responded enthusiastically, giving her a strong hug. "No wonder we take you with us wherever we go. Let's do this: I'll walk back and talk to Delos at the wheel, while you two wander down the deck and stop above Carlos's cabin."

"All right," David said, turning.

Mark leaned over to Penny and whispered in her ear.

"After all, the crew expects you and David to get rid of me so you two can be alone!"

She stomped vigorously on his foot, and he yelled out, "Hey!"

"What's wrong, Mark?" David asked, turning back quickly.

"Nothing, David. He just put his foot in his mouth again, and hurt himself. He'll recover. Let's go." She took his arm and urged him down the deck.

Mark laughed as he hobbled off toward the stern, favoring his foot. He hurried so as to get ahead of Penny and David, climbed the steps to the quarterdeck, and greeted Delos, the stocky quiet man at the wheel.

David and Penny wandered casually down the starboard side of the ship, seemingly in no hurry, and came to a stop at the rail. "Is this near his cabin?" Penny asked quietly.

"I guess not," David answered. "I can't hear any voices. Let's wait here a minute, then wander a bit farther."

They waited for a moment, looking over the side as if engrossed in their conversation. Then David straightened, and the two walked a little farther down the deck.

Right away, David knew they'd hit the jackpot! That's when they heard the voices of Carlos and Lycenus from below. They'd left the port open, as had everyone else, and seemed to have no idea that their conversation carried to the deck just above them.

"They're speaking German!" Penny said in a low voice.

"Right," David replied. "I bet they think no one on board can understand them. Let me listen."

David's mother had begun teaching him German when he was five years old and the family had moved to Germany. He'd kept it up all through his school years; now he was fluent. Standing just above their open port, he could easily hear what the men were saying.

"I'll drink to that!" Carlos said exuberantly. The sound of clinking glasses followed. They were toasting something, apparently, David figured. Then he heard Lycenus reply.

"We've done it, Carlos! We've done it! All these years we've planned. Now it's paid off!"

Carlos laughed in return. "We have indeed! But you gave me a real scare when you insisted that we call the harbormaster and demand that he inspect the ship! I just knew that would sink us! Why didn't he find the art in those barrels?"

David's heart stood still! He thought, *The art is in those barrels! We were right! That's what had happened!* He strained to hear Lycenus's answer.

"Because I packed those barrels myself," Lycenus boasted. "I designed them with a false bottom—rather, with a false half-barrel! The top was filled with bricks for the ship's ballast, just as our papers show. The bottom of those barrels has the ancient gold masks and cups and jewelry. The only ones who knew were the two men who helped me."

"Where are those two now?" Carlos asked curiously. "The TV said they had disappeared also."

"Disappear they did!" Lycenus laughed. "Into the mountains of Italy! We've planned this for two years, Carlos. They've gotten an advance payment—a handsome payment—and they'll get more when we get ours. They left as soon as the security cavalcade took the dummy shipment to the dock, and they scampered out of the country. They'll never be found."

"But how did you adjust the plan when the security people came aboard the freighter to inspect the barrels bound for London? I thought that would ruin everything!"

"No adjustment was necessary, Carlos. I'd timed our departure on this galley—with the nation's televisions beaming us all over Greece—to coincide with the shipment to London. It gave me a scare for a minute, frankly. The security company had said nothing about a surprise inspection! But we were already here on board the galley with the barrels of treasures. All I had to do was call the harbormaster and insist he inspect our vessel."

"It was a close call!" Carlos insisted.

"That it was, Carlos, that it was! But we made it. Think of the expression on the security people's faces when they opened those barrels looking for ancient art and found bricks!" He laughed.

"What a plan, Andropous! What a plan! I always said you inherited all the brains in the family. Now you've proved it. Here's to you!"

There was silence for a few moments as the men enjoyed their victory celebration. David felt sick. How would they get out of this?

Andropous Lycenus spoke again. "Actually, Carlos, you had as much to do with this as I. You picked the trustworthy crewmen; you got rid of most of Alexander Spirodes's own crew; you wormed yourself into his favor—you've got to tell me that story! You made this end of it work."

"Well, as you know, the police think I'm dead," Carlos replied. "I was in Romania when I got your signal. Incidentally, that American girl Mr. Spirodes brought on board asked about my English accent. She recognized it as different. I made the mistake of telling her I'd learned English with my brother in England one year. I wasn't about to tell her that you and I learned that language in a KGB intelligence school in East Germany! But she lives in Africa and knows how people speak in England."

"No harm done," Lycenus said casually. "We've seen them for the last time! The catamaran joins us at midnight. We'll lock everyone in their cabins while they sleep—you've done a great job with those door handles! And she'll never hear your voice again."

"When do we meet the submarine?" Carlos asked eagerly.

"Half an hour after leaving the galley. They'll intercept us and take on the barrels."

"How will the sub find us on this dark sea?" Carlos asked, intrigued.

"Carlos, this is a high-tech operation from beginning to end! That sub is on a special mission for Admiral Zukhov, head of the Russian Black Sea Fleet! They're following us by satellite now and they know exactly where we are. The catamaran is following a few miles away. They've got us on their radar, beyond the reach of the set on this ship. After the catamaran makes contact and we transfer the barrels, we'll make a right angle turn and head straight south for 30 minutes. The sub will find us with no trouble at all. She'll surface right beside us!"

Carlos laughed with the beauty of the plan. "So the catamaran joins us at midnight and its crew helps us transfer the barrels to their deck. We leave the galley's crew locked in their cabins and the ship sailing with the automatic steering to keep it on course. What a joke on Mr. Spirodes! He'll have to smash his way out of his own cabin on his precious ancient ship!"

"Think what this haul will mean to our intelligence operations around the world!" Lycenus said, changing the subject. "This art will bring hundreds of millions on the black market in Asia! The cowards in Moscow have given in to those capitalist peasants and slashed the budget of our KGB. But with this sale, we'll be able to finance our work again. We'll be able to prepare for the restoration of our Communist Empire when this soft democratic experiment fails. What a deed we've done for international socialism!"

"What a role we're playing in history! To think—two Greek peasant boys have changed the world!" Carlos's voice was thick now. He'd had a lot to drink, David concluded.

"Let's turn in for a couple of hours," Lycenus said. "We'll be rested when the catamaran comes. Wake me up at half past eleven."

"All right, brother," Carlos said.

David took Penny's hand and led her swiftly toward the quarterdeck, where they joined Mark and Delos. The Greek knew a bit of English and enjoyed talking with the friendly Americans. After a few minutes, the three wandered again toward the bow of the ship.

David told Mark and Penny what he had heard. They were astounded!

"So they'll board us at midnight from a catamaran!" Mark said, awed. "Do you think it's that big black one we saw in the harbor?"

"I'm sure it is!" Penny replied. "They were very interested in us when I took their picture! Several men were staring at us, and at the galley, through their binoculars. I'm sure that's the one!"

"And Mr. Spirodes told us how fast it goes—faster than we can! And that it can hold a large cargo," David added.

"What will we do?" Penny asked.

"We'll tell Mr. Spirodes first," Mark said. "We've got to let him know."

Just then Carlos came up from below, spoke with the man at the wheel, and strolled casually forward, joining them at the bow.

"How do you like our voyage?" he asked in his friendly way.

"We love it!" Penny replied. "But we're about to go to bed. I think we're worn out just by being passengers!"

Carlos laughed his hearty laugh. "That's what the ocean does to you!"

He turned and walked back along the deck, then took the steps to the level below. The three walked slowly after him.

"I'll go see if Mr. Spirodes is still awake," Mark said. "You two stay on deck until I talk with him. That way, we won't all be missed at the same time."

Penny and David leaned against the starboard rail, looking at the dark sea, speaking softly, waiting for Mark to return. When he did, his voice was tense.

"Carlos was standing outside Mr. Spirodes's cabin. When I started to knock on the door, he told me that he'd already gone to sleep and asked if he could help me. I told him it wasn't urgent, that I just had a question, but it could wait until morning."

"How will we reach Mr. Spirodes?" Penny asked, alarmed now.

"I don't know," Mark answered, his voice troubled. "When I came back here, Carlos went into his cabin, but he left the door open. He's keeping an eye on things."

"Then we won't be able to talk to Mr. Spirodes about this?" she asked. Were they entirely on their own?

"Not without causing a lot of suspicion in Carlos's mind," Mark replied, "and that could cause trouble we'd rather avoid."

David spoke up. "Mark, it's 9:30 now. We've got two hours before Carlos and Lycenus plan to get up and prepare for the catamaran. Couldn't you and I get into the hold—it's not locked—and move those barrels across the deck? They all look alike. We could swap the ones with the art, on the right side of the ship, with those on the left. That way, the men from the catamaran would take the wrong barrels, but they wouldn't know it."

"But what if you got caught?" Penny said in alarm. "Carlos or Lycenus, or some of the crew, could catch you."

"Not if they're all asleep," David said. "We can sneak in,

swap the barrels, then sneak back to our cabins."

Mark pondered his friend's plan, weighing the dangers.

"Isn't there any other way?" Penny asked, deeply alarmed at the danger that faced the boys. "I hate to think of you two being caught in that hold. There's no telling what those men might do."

"Well," David reasoned, "we can't get past Carlos to wake Mr. Spirodes. This way, we at least have a chance to save the art without attracting attention. Then we can all go to sleep and let them lock us in our cabins. We'll take a crowbar from that storage cabinet in the passageway and break out of our rooms after they leave on the catamaran."

"I think that's the only thing we can do, David," Mark said deliberately. He'd thought of other ways but didn't see any worth trying.

"How can I help?" Penny asked.

"You can keep watch," David answered. "If you stand in the passageway, you can cough to warn us. We'll hear you and get out the other end. Otherwise we won't know if anyone is heading our way."

"Won't the crew hear you if you go past their cabins?" she asked.

"Not if they're asleep," David replied. "And we've got tennis shoes."

"You know what?" Mark asked suddenly. "I just remembered something. This gives us another option! I think we can crawl in and out through those portholes. They're not big, but I got my shoulders through earlier when I tried to look up at the masts. I think we could climb along the railing on the side of the ship, get to the forward part of the deck, and go into the hold from the stairs near the bow! No one would see us leave our cabins. And we could come back the same way!"

"That's great!" David said. "Then we can appear to go to our rooms first, and sneak out later to reach the hold!"

Penny's heart was deeply troubled. What if someone found that the boys were not in their room and alerted Carlos? What if someone discovered them while they were transferring the cargo from one side of the ship to the other? And how would Mark and David climb out of their portholes—right over the ocean—and get to the deck above? If they did that, could they climb back? They were taking awful chances. She shuddered at the danger that was closing in on them.

The sky grew even darker as they went below. The wind was cold.

The boys decided to stay in Penny's cabin that night, for they didn't want her to be alone with strange men boarding the ship. With troubled hearts the three shut themselves in her room.

CHAPTER 8

THE SWAP

Time to go," David said, checking his watch, then turning off the slender minimag flashlight that hung from the lanyard around his neck. He tucked it inside his polo shirt.

"Oh, please, let's pray first," Penny said.

"We sure will," her brother replied. In the dark cabin the three prayed in turn. Then Penny reached out and gave each a hug. "Please be careful!"

"I'll go first," Mark insisted. "After all, this climb along the deck was my idea."

Grudgingly, David let Mark take the lead. Both boys were stiff and sore from lying cramped on the floor between Penny's bunk and the wall. Standing on the cabin's one chair, which he'd placed just under the rectangular porthole, Mark slowly and quietly opened the glass to the dark night. Then he stuck his head and shoulders through, twisted up, and reached for the wooden rail that ran the length of the ship, just under the wooden canopy that protected the oarsmen from enemy archers. He found a good grip and slowly pulled himself out.

The water below was rougher now. Mark could feel the splash of waves occasionally, as he grabbed the rails with hands and feet and proceeded to climb horizontally along the outside of the ship's hull, his body hanging over the water. His tennis shoes made no sound as they reached for a grip around the regular wooden posts that supported the rail overhanging the side of the galley.

David followed him out. Then Penny found herself alone in the cabin, staring out at the pitch-dark night and sea, straining to hear the boys as they inched themselves along the ship's side toward the bow.

What if one of the crew is leaning at the rail as they pass? she wondered. *What if Carlos comes up early and finds them?* Tormented with thoughts of the dangers the boys faced, she leaned her head against the ship's bulkhead and prayed earnestly for their safety.

The boys labored along the side of the ship, making no sound, gripping with their arms and their legs. Every minute they expected to hear footsteps or voices above them.

But they heard nothing except the sound of waves as the galley plowed through the sea and the sound of the wind as it whistled through the rigging above the deck.

Finally Mark reached the spot they'd chosen. He stopped and lifted his head slowly to look over the railing above. One false move, one mistaken act, and he'd be discovered! Raising his head slowly above the rail, he strained to see through the darkness. Were any of Carlos's crew nearby? He saw no one. Nor could he hear any sound of men on deck. Looking back to his left, he made out the dim form of David's body clinging to the side of the ship.

Here goes, he said to himself. Slowly he climbed over the railing, keeping his body as low as possible, and slid to the deck. David followed him. Then the two crept across the passage to the opening that led to the hold below. After crawling over the wooden cowling placed above the steps to the lower deck, they slowly descended the steps to the black passage below.

Taking out the minimag from inside his polo shirt, Mark flashed it quickly ahead of him and saw the door to the hold. His rubber-soled tennis shoes made no sound as he moved across the deck to the door. Feeling for the handle, he turned it slowly, opened the door, and stepped inside, David followed, closing the door quietly behind him.

Mark flashed his light around the hold. There were the barrels! Two rows on each side of the hold, six barrels to a row. To his left as he faced the stern of the ship were the ones with the stolen treasure, the ones the men from the catamaran would soon steal! These had red ropes around their tops.

David bent his head close to Mark. "We'll need to use a light—I'll stick mine on the floor between those barrels, so it won't show too much."

He placed the minimag on the deck, but shone it back toward the wall so that most of its light was hidden. The boys could see well enough to work, but that was all.

"Look at these red ropes looped around the barrels with the art," Mark whispered. "We've got to change these when we swap the barrels."

"Those are the ones Carlos said were filled with bricks, for ballast," David whispered, pointing to his right. "The ones farther back have ship's stores."

They went to work. First they lifted off the heavy rope that stretched from ringbolts in the walls to circle each barrel. Then they gripped one of the barrels and rolled it slowly over the narrow wooden railing on the deck that kept the cargo from sliding. They then rolled the barrel into the passage between the two rows of stores and set it down.

They returned for the barrel behind it, next to the ship's side, and rolled this also into the passage between the rows. Then they lifted the ropes from the barrels on the right of the ship—the ones with the stolen art—and slowly eased the first two across the deck. They rolled these into the places just vacated by the barrels on the other side. The barrels filled with bricks were heavy and difficult to move and the boys were sweating after they'd rolled them into the place of the two that held the ancient Greek art.

"That's two of them!" Mark sighed gratefully. "Just ten more to go." In the dim light cast by the almost hidden flashlight, David could just see the brave grin on his friend's face. He grinned back.

They tackled the next two barrels of bricks, tilting them, rolling them with difficulty across the deck, setting them in the passage between. The process continued. David looked at the luminous dial of his watch. It was taking longer than they had thought it would.

Back in her cabin, Penny waited for 15 minutes, as they'd

planned. Then she went to the door, listened, and eased it open with infinite care. She was wearing her bathrobe, but was dressed in shirt and shorts underneath. Her task was to go down the hall to the bathrooms, which were at the midsection, just where the hall turned from one side of the ship to the other. From here, she'd be able to notice anyone else coming down the hall. If she heard someone, she would cough to warn the boys, then go into one of the bathrooms.

Fearfully she crept down the dimly lit hall, eased open the door of one of the bathrooms—there were two, separated by two showers at this part of the ship—and stood waiting. The rising and falling of the ship as it plowed through the seas, the creaking of the wood, the strange sounds and smells, and the overriding sense of the danger they faced—all these filled her heart with fear. Again she prayed.

Then she waited. And waited. The ship rolled gently as it plowed through the darkened waters.

Four miles to the south, the black catamaran swept across the sea with incredible ease, seeming to fly above the water rather than cut through it. The black sails above the black hull made it invisible in the dark night.

The skipper had decided to ease closer to the galley. "We could get a head start on transferring the stores," he'd told his executive officer. He was scanning his radarscope with care as he followed the course of the galley and plotted his own approach.

"We don't want to warn Mr. Spirodes," his exec said.

"No danger of that," the skipper replied. "He'll be unconscious! Our man is at the wheel—and the radarscope—of the galley. The others won't have any idea that we're here."

The men on board went about their business with quiet and well-drilled efficiency. Four of them were using acetylene torches, cutting square panels in the top of the twin hulls.

"Let's just hope that we don't meet any rough seas after they cut away our top deck," the exec said anxiously. He'd never liked this part of the plan.

"Nothing to worry about," the skipper said, taking his pipe from his mouth and spitting over the side. "Those panels will be cut on three sides only; the fourth side will be cut when we reach the sub. We've got to have this boat ready to sink just as soon as we transfer the barrels to the sub! The explosive charges will blow out the bottom, but if we don't cut away the top of the decking, this thing will float and be found.

"The whole point of this plan is that there will be no evidence left! We'll put the cargo on the sub and sink this catamaran! Nothing will remain, no clue at all, to tell the police what happened to the barrels on the ship.

"What a plan!" he marveled, puffing at his pipe again. "What a plan! Nothing will connect the galley's cargo with the art taken from the museum! There's no clue! Once we're on the sub, we'll be under the sea, on the way to the transport ship that will take the treasures from the sub to Hanoi. No one will ever know what happened!" He chuckled at the slick scheme.

He puffed again on his pipe and spat over the side. Then he laughed out loud at the thought of what they were getting away with. And he began in his mind to spend the money he'd get for his part.

"Don't let those men cut all the deck!" the captain said sharply, as his mind came suddenly back to the present. "They've got to leave room for the pumps!"

"I'll check on that!" the exec said, leaving the cabin.

The catamaran swept swiftly across the darkened sea under the huge black sail, skimming across the waves, drawing steadily closer to the galley.

Back on the galley, the tension in the ship's hold was increasing; David and Mark were almost through.

"Just two left!" David said. "It's not only that these barrels are heavy," he said quietly to Mark. "It's the strain of keeping so quiet while we move them that's wearing me out!"

"Me, too," Mark agreed. They were both drenched with sweat, but dared not pause for a moment.

"We can't leave Penny in that passage a minute longer than we have to!" David said, as they wrestled with another barrel.

Penny had waited, and waited, and waited. She kept looking at the watch she'd borrowed from Mark. Five minutes passed. Then 10. Then 15. Finally, she began to relax. *They must be almost through*, she said to herself. *Oh, it's almost over!*

The door opened down the hall and a man's bare feet stepped into the passage.

Heart racing suddenly, Penny coughed twice, then entered the bathroom and closed the door.

Had the boys heard her warning? Maybe the man was only coming to the bathroom. But what she feared was a sudden inspection of the hold while the boys were transferring the barrels. Penny began to tremble. She prayed.

She heard a man enter the bathroom next to the adjoining shower. *Did they hear me cough?* she asked herself anxiously.

They had. "Quiet, Mark!" David had whispered urgently.

The boys froze. The barrel in their hands was tilted on its side as they'd been rolling it across the passage. Now they held it in place at this awkward angle, not moving, hardly breathing, wondering why Penny had sent the warning. Was someone coming to the hold, or just to the bathroom?

After several minutes had passed, the boys heard a tap on the door. It opened, and Penny stuck her head into the near-darkness. "He's gone back to his cabin," she whispered. "Are you almost finished?"

"Almost!" Mark whispered back. "You go to your room. We'll be there in just a minute."

"Can't you come back by the hall?" she asked.

"We can," Mark answered. "Get back quick—we're almost through!"

Reassured, Penny closed the door and moved quietly down the hall to her cabin. Easing open the door, she went in, closed the door behind her, and sank thankfully on the bed. She was exhausted, but the job was done! Now all she had to do was wait for the boys to return.

Slowly the tension drained out of her. Waves of relief

followed. They had done it! They'd swapped the treasures for the ship's stores! They'd saved the priceless art of ancient Greece!

Suddenly she heard a click of metal on metal at her door. Startled, she sat up, heart pounding, terribly alert. But she heard nothing else. Were Mark and David trying to get in? She knew she'd left the door unlocked for them. They'd agreed to gather in her room and stay with her until the catamaran and its crew had left.

Quietly she rose, moved in the darkness to the door, groped carefully for the handle, turned slowly, and pulled.

Nothing happened. She pulled harder. The door didn't move. It was locked from the outside! Someone had shut her in. Now Mark and David would not be able to come back through the passage. They were too late! Would they be trapped in the hall as they returned? And she was alone— the very thing the boys had sought to avoid.

Heart pounding, her mind reeling, she struggled to gather her thoughts. Would they still be able to crawl back the way they'd come? She got up and went to the open porthole.

Looking out, she was startled to see the dark shape of a sailing vessel about to hit the galley! She ducked instantly and sat on the bunk. Then she heard lines thrown across from deck to deck. Huddled in her cabin, terribly alone, she prayed for Mark and David.

Forward in the ship's hold, the boys had finished. "That's the last one!" David said gratefully, as they eased the barrel into place. "Now let's put back the red ropes on the barrels of bricks, and let those thieves have them!"

Swiftly the boys placed the ropes around the tops of the barrels they'd moved. "Let's go," David said, switching off his light and moving toward the door through which Penny had spoken to them. They could go to their cabin that way and save themselves the agonizing climb along the side of the ship.

Suddenly they heard voices outside the door they were about to open! The voices were not loud—but they were speaking in German!

"Quick!" David whispered urgently as he whirled around. "Back! We've got to go back the way we came!"

They raced on silent feet to the other end of the cargo hold. Behind them, they heard the door open.

CHAPTER 9

BOARDED!

There it is!" the executive officer said as the black catamaran sped toward the galley at 18 knots.

"And to think the brave Alexander Spirodes is lying drugged in his cabin!" the skipper laughed. "Carlos drugged their coffee. Mr. Spirodes has only two men who are loyal to him. He thinks they all are, but Carlos brought his own crew with him. So Mr. Spirodes and his men won't wake up for hours! Then they'll find themselves locked in their cabins." He laughed, puffed his pipe in self-satisfaction, and spat into the sea.

The exec laughed with him. Their plan was foolproof!

"Prepare to board!" the skipper said sharply to the six men beside him. They were dressed in black, wore rubber-soled shoes, and carried submachine guns in their hands. Each had been carefully briefed; each knew what to do. First, they'd help Carlos secure the ship and make sure the crew were locked in their cabins. Then they'd help Carlos and his crew transfer the treasures from the galley's hold to the catamaran. Carlos would rip out the radio of the galley—there'd be no way for Mr. Spirodes to call for help.

69

Looking continually toward the galley as the ships closed, the skipper saw two men at the steering tiller. One flashed his light again. A third man was midships, waiting with a line to secure the approaching catamaran so they could transfer the cargo.

It was beautifully done. The catamaran swept closer, dropped its sail to the deck, altered course, and came beside the galley with just two yards of space between them. Then the catamaran's engines powered the boat as it kept pace with the galley. Both ships were moving at the slow pace of six knots, just as planned.

The black-clad men from the catamaran leaped to the deck of the galley, fanned out, and raced to join Carlos's men.

Below deck, Carlos and his brother, Andropous Lycenus, had entered the ship's hold. Because their flashlight was focused on the deck before them, they didn't see the boys leave through the other door. There was no light in the far hall to give the boys away. But Carlos heard something.

"Was that a door closing?" he asked sharply in German, raising the beam to the door just as it closed.

"Probably not," his brother replied. He was behind Carlos and hadn't heard the faint sound. "Check the barrels with the art!"

Obediently Carlos flashed his light to their right as the two men walked swiftly forward toward the double row of barrels with the red ropes. "There they are!" Carlos said excitedly. "What a beautiful sight! Andropous, you're a genius!"

"True, but I've had a lot of help!" his brother answered.

"Let's go topside and greet the catamaran."

They continued forward, stepped quickly out the door from which the boys had just exited, and climbed the steps to the deck. Here they turned to their right and headed rapidly toward midships where one of their men waited, watching the approaching catamaran.

"What perfect timing!" Carlos said admiringly. "When they signaled they wanted to board us a half hour earlier than we'd planned, I wondered if they'd make it. But they did."

"I told you this was high tech!" his brother said laughing as he slapped Carlos on the back. "We've got the instruments to do anything we want these days! Remind me to tell you how much money we've spent on this project!"

Just a moment before, Mark and David had rushed from the hold ahead of the two men. They'd crept cautiously up the steps to the deck, and turned right to go over the rail and climb back to the cabin the way they'd come. Suddenly they saw in the darkness the dim shape of the approaching catamaran looming beside the galley! A light flashed from the catamaran.

"Back to the other side!" David whispered urgently. Quickly they dodged to the other side of the galley and crawled over the edge, hanging on to the wooden canopy that ran along that side also. Seconds later, Carlos and Andropous emerged from the hatch and went to the opposite side of the ship.

Peering through a gap in the rails to which he clung, Mark saw the men leap from the catamaran and fan out over the deck of the galley. "We can't get back the way we came!"

Mark whispered in alarm as they hung by their hands and feet.

"Penny's in her room alone!" David whispered back, anguish in his tone. "But we can't get to her room with that catamaran there!"

"Carlos has probably locked all the cabin doors by now," Mark replied. "That's what you heard him say he was going to do. So we've got no other place to go. Their men will be all over the deck while they transfer the barrels."

"But they can't see us under this part of the canopy," David said hopefully. "We'll have to hang on until they finish the job and leave."

"Let's hope no one comes looking over this side," Mark replied.

The two boys held themselves to the ship by hands and feet, praying. The slow speed of the galley had changed the effects of the sea on the boat, increasing the pitching and plunging. Waves splashed up from below and drenched them both. Their minds were in turmoil. How long would those men take to put the barrels on the catamaran? Could they hold on long enough?

Gathering the black-clad men and two of his own, Carlos led them below quickly. Turning on the ceiling lights in the hold, he took them to the barrels with the red ropes around them. "There they are! Get them out of here!"

"How quiet do we have to be?" one of the black-clad men from the catamaran asked him.

"Don't worry about being quiet," Carlos laughed. "Mr. Spirodes and his two men are doped. They won't wake up for hours! Three American teenagers are locked in their cabins; you can forget about them!"

The men laughed and went to work. Removing the red ropes, they rolled the barrels into the passage, toward the steps leading up to the deck above. A crewman had just placed a ramp over the steps. Then he threw down a rope sling and the men rolled the first barrel into this.

"Take it away," one called, and the men above hauled it quickly up the ramp, rolled it out of the sling, and began to roll it along the right side of the ship to the rail.

Here, amidships, the loading port of the rail had been unlocked and swung back. A ramp had been thrown from the deck of the catamaran to the deck of the galley. Two men rolled the barrel across this to the catamaran, where it was taken and stored. The other barrels came up from the hold in quick succession and were swiftly moved across.

"This is going faster than we had thought," the skipper of the catamaran said to his exec. "What teamwork!"

Carlos went back to the radio room beside Alex's cabin and systematically wrecked the equipment. Coming up again, he called across to the catamaran: "These men will be silent as the tomb—even when they wake! I've destroyed their radio!" He laughed his booming laugh.

The skipper laughed back and puffed on his pipe. What an operation! And what a wad they'd get for pulling this off!

Fourteen minutes after the catamaran had come alongside, the last barrel crossed the ramp and was stacked beside the others.

"That's it!" Carlos said. "Let's clean up!"

The men in the hold brought up the ramp they'd attached

to the steps and took it to the catamaran. The cargo ramp was taken across also. The railing of the galley was swung back into place.

Swiftly the black-clad men leaped back to their ship as Carlos and Lycenus went below for a final check. The cabin doors were locked; no one could get out without breaking out. "Those kids are still quiet," Lycenus said.

"They're lazy American teenagers," Carlos replied. "I told you they didn't need anything to make them sleep!" He laughed aloud.

The two men came back on deck. "Let's go!" Carlos said to his waiting crewmen, as he ran for the quarterdeck. The crew crossed over at once. Carlos checked the speed of the galley; it was set at six knots. He checked the course, then set the automatic pilot to keep the ship on course. The galley should sail along for hours before Alex recovered his senses and broke out of his cabin.

"After you, Andropous, you genius!" he said to his brother. Laughing, the two men leaped across the ramp to the catamaran.

The skipper increased the catamaran's speed, changed course, and the big black craft sped swiftly away from the silent, pilotless galley.

CHAPTER 10

NO PLACE TO HIDE!

The noise of the men rolling barrels across the deck had ceased; so had the sound of their voices. But still the boys hung on to their precarious perch under the canopy on the left side of the galley. And still they were drenched by the cold waves from below.

"I think they've gone," David said quietly. His muscles were straining. Both boys had shifted positions as often as they could, changing their grip as well. But the strain was telling now.

"Let's wait a little longer," Mark cautioned.

The waves hit them again. They were soaked with salt water. But they waited.

"I'll take a look," David volunteered finally.

He lifted himself carefully, raising his head above the deck but still below the wooden canopy that ran the length of the ship from foredeck to quarterdeck. He could see nothing. Nor did he hear any voices.

"I can't make out the catamaran. Let's go," he said.

They climbed slowly over the railing and dropped to the deck. Their arms and legs ached from the strain and they

75

rested a few moments, regaining strength. Then they started to crawl around the platform at the base of the foremast. Reaching this, they looked toward the other side of the galley. The catamaran was gone!

Looking down the length of the galley, they couldn't make out any flashlights or signs of anyone moving around the deck. There was no sound but that of the waves hitting the ship and the wind whistling through the lines. They stood up, stretching gratefully.

"We'd still better be careful," David cautioned, as they began to move quietly down the length of the ship.

"And to think I used to do everything I could to get out of Dad's weight lifting plan!" Mark said. "I just hated it when I was younger!"

"Well, he sure didn't know we'd be doing this!" David replied.

"No, but he kept saying we'd have to be able to protect ourselves and our families," Mark admitted. "Boy, was he right!"

"Look!" David said suddenly, grabbing Mark's arm.

Peering over the right side of the ship they could barely make out the black smudge of the catamaran's sail against the night. Then they saw the running lights on the mast come on.

"Boy, that thing goes fast!" David said, awed at the vessel's sudden speed. "Let's get Penny!"

They ran down the steps and raced to her cabin.

David knocked urgently. "Penny," he called, "Let us in!"

They heard a cry from within. "I can't!" she said. "It's

locked from outside!"

"That's right!" David remembered. He fumbled with the bolts around the door handle, but couldn't open it in the darkness. Taking out the minimag from within his shirt, he flashed it on the door. Then he could see how the curved bolt had been put into the clamps made for it. Pulling it out he yanked open the door.

She flew into his arms. "Oh, I didn't know what had happened to you!" she said through her tears.

"We got away just ahead of Carlos, and crawled over the left side of the deck. We've been holding on since then!"

Penny released David, threw her arms around Mark's neck, and hugged him, too. "Oh, thank God you're safe!"

"We have—and we do!" he said, hugging her fiercely. "Boy, are we glad you're O.K.!" He'd never tell anyone how anxious he'd been for her while he'd hung helplessly over the sea.

"We can't show a light," David said suddenly. "We don't want to let the catamaran know anyone's loose. I'll see if I can wake Mr. Spirodes."

Mark and Penny followed David as he carefully shielded his small flashlight, aiming it on the deck before them until they reached Mr. Spirodes's cabin. He removed the curved bolt that held the door, and the three of them went inside. Flashing the light on the bed, they saw Alexander Spirodes, unconscious on his bunk.

David went over and shook the man. "He's out of it!" he said to the others. "We heard them say they'd drugged the coffee. They won't wake up for hours, Carlos said."

"Hours!" Penny cried. "What will we do, then?"

"Let's think about it," Mark said. "We'd better go back on deck. At least we can keep an eye on things there." They hurried back up the steps to the deck and peered into the darkness to the right of their course.

"I can't see the catamaran," Mark said, staring into the darkness. "Can you?"

"No," David answered. "Can you, Penny?"

"No, we can't see anything more than a hundred yards away."

"But they could have powerful night glasses and see us," David warned. "Infrared binoculars can see a long way in the dark. We'd better stay low."

They sat down on the deck behind the rail, huddling together, waiting. Half an hour passed.

"Will the catamaran come back?" Penny asked finally.

"Not unless they find out they've got the wrong barrels," Mark answered.

"They probably don't have time to open them now," David said, "but they will when they get on the submarine. Maybe we should change course and head away from them."

They thought about that in silence. But the more they did, the more convinced David became.

"We've got to change course!" he said finally. "We've got to get as far away from here as we can! Let's check the radar to see if they're out of range. We don't want them to notice us changing direction."

They ran up the steps to the quarterdeck and crowded around the radarscope just beside the wheel. "I don't see anything on the scope," Mark said.

The boys discussed the course they should steer. "The catamaran was going directly away from us," Mark remembered.

"That would be almost due south," David suggested. "We're heading between the Cyclades and Crete now, I think. But we don't know this ocean at all."

"We'd better just reverse course, then," Mark said, "and head back to the west."

"Boy!" David exclaimed. "What a mess! Our first trip on a real ocean and the crew is unconscious! How in the world did we get into this?"

"But Mr. Spirodes let both you boys steer the boat," Penny reminded them. "He let you change speed, too. You can do it!"

"He sure did," Mark said. "But steering for an hour in daylight with the captain beside you is one thing. Groping for a new course in the dark, trying to escape a submarine, is another!"

"Let's turn around now," David said. "That's the safest thing to do. If we put the throttle at top speed, we'll make some distance. Besides, they might not find us even if they do discover that we swapped the barrels." David wasn't too sure about that statement. He thought a submarine could find anything within a great distance with its powerful radar and sonar. But he wanted to encourage the others as well as himself. Peering at the illuminated compass, he saw their heading. Flipping the switch, he threw off the automatic steering and took the wheel.

"We're only going six knots!" Mark exclaimed in surprise. "No wonder the seas felt different! I'll put the throttle on full speed!" He did so.

David turned the wheel and the galley began to swerve to the left.

At once the seas buffeted the galley, causing it to pitch and roll. Ignoring the pitching, David kept it in a gentle turn, swinging around to the north, then to the west, watching the compass needle move. Now they were heading directly away from their former direction.

The ship was picking up speed. "We'll be 15 miles from here in an hour," David said.

"And that sub might be 30 miles away from the spot where we turned before they discover that they've got the wrong barrels!" Mark said hopefully. "That is, if they inspect them."

"Even if they do discover they've been tricked, they'd still have to find us," David said. "The Mediterranean's pretty big!"

"Yes, but there's no place to hide on the sea," Penny said soberly.

The boys didn't say anything. What she said was true. On the sea, there's no place to hide.

CHAPTER 11

THE GOLF-II BALLISTIC MISSILE SUBMARINE

The submarine was old, too old for active duty, Captain Stokowski knew, and too old for a first-class submariner like himself to command. He deserved one of the new Akula subs—those quiet, deadly stalkers of the sea that could give the American Los Angeles ships a run for their money.

But he'd made a mistake—on shore, of all places. He'd criticized the umpires' decision in a naval war game. He'd insisted that the American anti-sub planes would catch the Soviet submarines before the subs could attack the American ships; unless, that is, they plotted a different attack course than the one they'd planned in the exercise room.

And he knew his facts. He'd told the war-game umpires, and the competing captains, of the range of the American electronic gear. He'd shown them that the umpires around the table had been foolishly optimistic in awarding the victory to

81

the Russian subs.

"We'll be killed before we can locate and attack them," he'd insisted.

He had been overruled. Now he was captain of an obsolete Golf-II diesel-powered ballistic missile submarine, one of the oldest in the Soviet arsenal, one that had been decommissioned in the latter part of 1990 and only recently resurrected for a series of special missions. Just over 300 feet long, displacing 2,900 tons, this Golf-II had been converted twice: first, to a missile testing boat, and next, to a vessel used for various auxiliary jobs, such as the one it was on now.

What a stupid job this was for a ballistic missile submarine commander like himself! To stalk a *civilian* catamaran, to meet it at a predetermined time, at a predetermined place on the sea, then to take aboard a dozen barrels of cargo. A dozen barrels of cargo! Then to proceed submerged to the eastern end of the Mediterranean. There, they'd transfer this strange freight to a transport ship flying the Liberian flag!

There was a knock on the door of his tiny cabin. "Come in!" he shouted.

"We've arrived, Captain," the exec said. The executive officer knew the moods of his captain, and he understood the reason for them. He didn't blame him, and he didn't get angry at the captain's outbursts. "The catamaran's right above us."

"All right," Captain Stokowski said, rising wearily. "Bring her up."

He followed the exec to the conning tower and stood quietly while the exec brought the ship to periscope depth.

Taking the periscope when it rose, the captain stooped, looked into the eyepiece, and moved his body swiftly around in a circle, sweeping the dark horizon, looking for other ships. Only the dark blur of the catamaran 50 yards to port caught his eye.

"Nothing else on our screens?" he asked, looking through the lens.

"Nothing, Captain," the officer of the deck replied.

"Bring her to the surface," he said, stepping back.

The exec gave the orders in a quiet tone. *This may be the oldest resurrected obsolete sub in the Russian Navy,* Captain Stokowski thought, *but it's certainly going to do its job if I have anything to do with it.* The sub rose to the surface.

Lookouts raced up the ladder of the conning tower and took their places in the unusually elongated structure that rose from the deck of the small submarine. The captain followed, turning his binoculars at once to the dark smudge that was the catamaran. He gave his orders quietly to the sailor beside him, who relayed them to the men below. Slowly the sub changed course, angling toward the catamaran.

"Give the recognition signal," Captain Stokowski commanded.

Another sailor flashed his light at the sailing ship. A light flashed back, several times, then flashed again.

"That's the code, Captain," the sailor said.

"Tell them to maintain course 095. We will come alongside at seven knots."

The message was flashed to the catamaran.

"They acknowledge, Captain."

"Very good. Prepare the hatch to receive the cargo."

Now the sub was drawing alongside the catamaran. The captain could see men on its deck and hear their voices. Suddenly he observed lights on the bows of the twin hulls.

"Put out those lights, you fools!" he shouted in a rage. Did they want to bring themselves to the attention of all the NATO ships in the Mediterranean?

"Yes, Captain," a voice replied over the water. The ships were now only 15 yards apart. "We're just cutting away the tops of our decks so this vessel will sink when we blow out the hulls. We're almost through."

"You're through now!" Captain Stokowski roared back. "Put out those torches!"

Cursing, the catamaran's skipper ordered his men to stop cutting away the last edge of the panels on the top of the hulls. *It's almost finished anyway*, he thought. But what an arrogant fool that sub skipper was to interfere with the work of another captain!

The catamaran and the submarine merged, ramps were thrown across the span between the two decks, and men began to roll the precious barrels rapidly from one ship to the other.

On the catamaran, Carlos was in fine humor. "We'll be under water in 10 minutes, the catamaran will be sunk without a trace, and there'll be no clues left at all!" he said to his brother. "What a coup! No one will ever know what happened to the art! No one will ever know where it went or who took it! This is one of the greatest heists in history! And we're getting away scot-free!" His booming laugh crossed the water to the submarine's bridge. Even Captain Stokowski relaxed and smiled. *This is going like clockwork,* he thought.

Several miles away, and thousands of feet above the surface of the sea, the electronics officer in the back of the big F-14 Tomcat stared at his radarscope.

"I've got a sub that's just surfaced, Charlie," he told his pilot. "It just came up beside that sailboat we spotted."

"A sub? Keep your eye on it, Bob," the pilot replied. "See what it does."

The powerful Grumman aircraft, loaded with electronic gear, weapons, and jet fuel, led the two plane-section in regular patrol around the perimeter of the carrier battle group below. Two Sparrow missiles and four Sidewinders hung beneath the swept-back wings of the incredible fighting machines. The six internal fuel tanks held 16,000 gallons. If they needed a longer range or more time in the air, the planes could be fitted with large external tanks, and they could be refueled again and again from planes sent up from the ship.

On the left side of the plane was the 20 millimeter cannon. Its shells, fired at the rate of 6,000 rounds a minute, could destroy not only enemy planes but also frigates and fleet destroyers.

But the electronic gear directed by the man in the backseat was more impressive than these weapons. Systems of active and passive recognition, powerful jamming instruments to destroy the electronic brains of enemy fighters and in-

coming missiles, superb sensors that picked up specks on the
ocean or on the desert and fed the data into the computer. This
data spoke volumes to the officer who played on the controls
of the equipment as a concert pianist plays on the ivory keys
of a grand piano. These, along with the weapons, the engines,
and the incredibly trained crews, made the U.S. Navy's
Tomcat an awesome and amazing fighting instrument.

There was nothing like it in the sky.

The two planes continued their routine patrol around
the perimeter of the battle group so far beneath them in the
darkness of the night sky. Bob watched the sub on his screen
it was 28,000 feet below them, miles and miles away. Fifteen
minutes passed.

"The sailboat's disappeared!" Bob said suddenly.

"What do you mean, 'disappeared'?" the pilot replied.
"It's got to be there. Want me to get closer?"

"That won't help. The thing's gone under."

"I'd better call the ship," Charlie said. "Those people
down there may need rescue." He radioed back to the aircraft carrier, the USS *Nimitz*, passed on the message, and
was told to investigate.

"Let's take a look," Charlie said, radioing his wingman to
follow him in a descending turn to the west. The big fighters
with their loads of fuel and missiles began to descend.

"Now the sub's gone!" Bob said, studying his scope with
astonishment.

"What's going on?" Charlie asked.

He moved the throttle and the giant fighter leaped ahead,
closely followed by its partner on the right. The planes

streaked downward, the mighty engines pouring on the power that hurtled them through the dark sky like giant missiles.

Far below, the submarine continued its dive. "Level off," Captain Stokowski ordered. Then he turned to his exec. "Take over. I'll meet those men in my cabin."

He was in a sour mood. What a way to end his distinguished naval career—picking up a dozen barrels and an equal number of crewmen from a catamaran! What had gotten into naval headquarters that would cause them to send even this obsolete sub to serve as a taxi for petty thieves? Sick at heart, he left the bridge and plodded somberly toward his small cabin where he'd ordered Carlos and his blond brother with the eye patch to wait for him. These were the men his orders told him were in charge of the cargo he'd just taken on board.

Ten minutes later Stokowski was a different man! Andropous Lycenus had ripped off his eye patch and spun a tale the likes of which the captain had never heard before!

Andropous told him briefly of the art in the National Archaeological Museum of Athens, the fabulous pieces of armor and jewelry from ancient history. "So, several years ago, my brother and I—"

"That was your idea, Andropous," Carlos interrupted. "I only tagged along and handled the nautical arrangements. You're the genius behind this operation."

"You're too kind, Carlos." His brother laughed with a modest wave of his hand, but he didn't deny the statement.

"Anyway, I learned of the plan to loan the art pieces to the British Museum in London. At once we—" His brother coughed accusingly. "All right! At once *I* thought that this was the chance of a lifetime!"

He paused dramatically. "But the problems were immense! The security in that museum is incredible! I know— I devised it! But when the director broached this plan to lend the art, I saw that we'd never have a better opportunity to steal it. So I took a brief leave and went at once to East Germany to visit Carlos."

"How can I ever forget that visit?" Carlos asked thoughtfully. "East Germany was the bleakest, most backward place I've ever seen! Four decades of socialism should have made a paradise out of the country. Instead, it was a wreck. And the collapse of the Soviet Union left us high and dry—and bankrupt. But you, Andropous, brought the dream back to life." He raised his glass toward his brother. Andropous bowed his head in acknowledgment.

"You brought back the dream," Carlos continued. "You showed us a way to gain a huge fortune. And with that fortune we could reestablish our intelligence networks, which have been so badly wrecked by these political changes. We could finance our agents again, finance their espionage operations, continue our work to destabilize the Western democracies. This will keep us going and keep the vision of socialism alive in Europe!"

"Carlos had fled Greece years ago," Andropous picked up the tale. "The police thought he was dead—we fed them that information—so he was the perfect man to manage the nautical side of this operation. He slipped back into Greece. I arranged his position with Alexander Spirodes through mutual contacts. Our network is still alive in every country, gentlemen! And Carlos got rid of some of the crew he found and replaced them with our men."

Then Captain Stokowski asked the question that had puzzled him. "But how in the world did you persuade the Russian navy to lend you this submarine, Andropous?"

"Carlos arranged that through his espionage network in East Germany," Andropous said with a broad smile. His face was flushed now, with the consciousness of the job he'd pulled off. "Carlos got the message to a core of faithful men in the KGB. They contacted Admiral Zukhov, of the Black Sea Fleet, and he arranged for you to meet us."

Carlos interrupted him then. "But, Andropous, this puzzles me, too. Surely even Admiral Zukhov can't take a sub from its duty and send it on any kind of mission he wants, can he?"

"Maybe I can fit that part together for you," Captain Stokowski said thoughtfully. "This sub is old, one of our oldest. In the seventies it had been one of our ballistic missile subs. But then more modern boats began to replace it and the others in its class. This sub began to be used for firing test missiles and for covert operations and other special assignments. It's been changed and modified out of all recognition. We don't even have search radar for picking up airplanes! We were being refitted when this mission came up, and we had to leave the dockyard before the ship was ready."

He shook his head and continued. "We have got sonar,

but it's mostly for navigation and for finding other boats like yours. But we're without weapons and modern equipment. We just take special loads like this one. So we're no longer a part of the navy's strategic force. Now we're under the direct operational command of Admiral Zukhov. Actually, Admiral Zukhov just sends us where he wants us."

The captain sat back in his chair. *Why, this is no trivial mission*, he thought. *This is the most important thing I've ever done for the navy and the Motherland!* He felt revived.

The admiral wasn't disciplining him by giving him this old sub and this strange assignment. This was an incredibly important strategic mission! Suddenly Captain Stokowski felt important again.

"And from just twelve barrels of old Greek artifacts we're going to get hundreds of millions of rubles?" he asked incredulously.

Andropous nodded.

Stokowski could hardly believe it. "What do these things look like that they would bring such a price?"

Andropous glanced across the small table at Carlos. "Let's show the captain," he said with his great laugh.

His brother nodded his agreement. "I'd like to see the stuff myself."

"Could you ask for two of our men to be brought here, Captain?" Andropous asked, leaning forward.

"Certainly," Stokowski replied. He spoke into the intercom: "Bring two of the Greek sailors to my cabin."

CHAPTER 12

FUGITIVES ON THE HIGH SEAS

The galley plowed through the Mediterranean Sea at top speed, rising and falling on the choppy waves, cleaving the darkness in a desperate attempt to put distance between itself and the Russian submarine.

Penny had gone below to make hot tea. Mark stood beside David at the wheel of the ship, peering first at the compass in its dim light, then at the radarscope, then ahead in the enveloping darkness.

"What time is it?" David asked.

Mark looked at the luminous dial of his watch. "Twenty-five after one."

"No wonder I'm so sleepy," David said.

"Want me to take the wheel?" Mark asked at once.

"Not yet," David replied. "I'm scared enough to steer for a while."

The two friends stood close together, awed by the dangers

they faced and the dangers to Penny. "I didn't want to scare Penny," David said at last, "but this is a long way from being over."

"I know it is," Mark replied grimly.

David continued. "We've got no way to stop a submarine from catching us, and if it does, we've got no way to stop those men from boarding this galley. What would they do to us if they found us trying to escape like this? They know that we know what they've done. They can't let us get away to tell anyone what happened."

They both digested this thought in silence.

"They'd probably take the barrels with the treasures and sink the galley and everyone on board," Mark said finally. "That's the only way they could make sure that no one reported what had happened. You're right; they can't let us get away now."

The ocean wind was colder. Both boys were chilled, their clothes still wet from the ocean spray that had hit them as they'd clung to the ship's side. An overcast sky blotted out the stars, and the moonless night enveloped them with its blackness. David steered by the dimly lit compass in front of the wheel.

"Here's something to cheer you guys up!" Penny's merry voice proclaimed as she stepped up to the deck with two steaming mugs on a tray. She set it on the platform beside the radarscope. "That's pretty strong tea! I thought you'd need it to stay awake!"

The black cold night seemed cheerier now that she'd joined them. Her joyful presence lifted their spirits. She stepped between them. "Can I get between you guys and stay warm? I'm freezing!"

"You sure can!" Mark answered, putting his arm around her waist. David put his arm around her shoulder and gave her a hug. She stood between the two young men, giving and receiving comfort and courage. She put her arm around Mark's waist and rested her head on David's shoulder. The three balanced together on the moving deck of the galley as it plowed its way into the blackness of the sea and the sky.

"David," Mark asked suddenly, "do you remember where Mr. Spirodes keeps the flares?"

"Yeah," David answered. "In the locker right behind us. He showed me that yesterday. The life jackets and the inflatable rubber raft and all the emergency gear are stored there. Maybe you should check that out. And get us some flashlights," he added.

"I'll get those first," Mark said. He left the bridge and groped his way down the steps to the deck below. Here he turned first to his cabin. Entering, he switched on the light and found his pack. He took his flashlight and then found David's as well. Turning off the light, he left his cabin and went to look at Mr. Spirodes and the two drugged crewmen.

Up on the deck, Penny snuggled closer to David in the warmth of his protecting arm. "I'm scared, David," she said in a small voice.

"We'll make it," he assured her, hugging her tighter. "We've got a good start on that sub, if it decides to come after us, which I doubt. They'll probably keep going; they've got no reason to suspect that the art has been switched from those barrels they took. I think we're safe." The wind blew her fine hair into his face. In other circumstances, he would have loved this moment.

Penny knew that he might be right. Those men might not look in the barrels. After all, they were the ones who'd put them on the galley. But she knew that she would look if she were in their place. She also knew that David was trying to keep her spirits up. She realized that that was her duty to him, too.

"I think you and Mark are so brave," she said truthfully. "I was really afraid when you left my cabin and crawled out over the ocean." She shuddered at the memory of the two of them hanging over the water as they climbed toward the entrance to the ship's hold.

"We were scared, too! And I didn't like that upside-down crawl over those seas!" he said with a laugh. In fact, he'd hated those moments, wondering if a strong wave would suddenly wash him and Mark off the ship.

He steered the ship with his right hand on the wheel, glancing down repeatedly at the compass before him. His strong left arm held her close. She closed her eyes and rested her head against his chest.

The wind was stronger now, roaring at them from their left, from the south, wrapping cold tendrils of fear around the ship.

"Don't forget your tea, David," she said suddenly.

"I won't," he said. But he didn't want to let her go. So he leaned his body against the wheel to keep it steady, then reached his right hand for the hot mug and took a hearty swig. "Boy, that's great!"

He set the mug down quickly, adjusted the course slightly, then leaned against the wheel again and took another gulp of tea.

"That makes everything seem better!" he said. "Well, that's not really true. *You* make everything better." He couldn't say more.

She looked up at him and smiled. They stood close together in growing peacefulness. Somehow, the darkness that enveloped them seemed less frightening.

"I've found our flashlights," Mark's voice announced as he came up the steps before them and reached the wheel. "Now let's see about those flares."

He went behind them to the wooden cabinet behind the wheel. There were two doors, each with brass handles. Opening these, he began to rummage within.

"Here they are!" he cried triumphantly. "Boy, this is great! There must be three dozen!"

"Maybe we'll see a ship or plane. Then we can send these flares up," David suggested hopefully. "There's got to be traffic in this part of the sea. If we can just get someone's attention, we'll have help."

"And here's a big flashlight," Mark added, bringing it out of the cabinet and setting it on the deck. "We could signal a long way with this. Now we're really equipped!"

He stood up and walked over to Penny and David. "How fast are we going?"

"Fourteen knots," David replied. "That's as fast as she'll do."

"That's plenty fast," Mark said. "In a couple of hours, we'll be a long way from where the catamaran left us. They'll never find us—if they come looking for us, that is. Frankly, I don't think they will. They've got no reason to open those barrels."

"What was in the barrels they took?" Penny asked curiously.

"Bricks," Mark answered. "The ones we substituted for the treasures were filled with bricks."

CHAPTER 13

THE TRICKSTERS TRICKED!

The submarine captain's cabin was now the scene of a hilarious victory celebration. Crewmen passing the door along the narrow corridor grinned at the wild noises from within.

Carlos's two seamen had come and received their instructions. Andropous had told them to open one of the barrels from the top and remove the stores packed inside, until they came to the next section, about a third of the way down.

"That's a false bottom," he said solemnly, with a broad wink. He told them how to open it. "Be careful! Bring us a couple of the things you find."

While they waited for the crewmen to return with the golden treasures, Andropous began to imagine what the reactions of the museum directors in Athens must have been when they first learned that the barrels on the ship heading for London contained not their precious treasures but—bricks! He pictured for Carlos and the captain the individual members of the board, telling of their achievements in business and politics.

"These are men who command, men who make things happen, men in charge!" he said. "They're the ones who put things over on others, who got where they are by outsmarting everyone in their way. They're the ones who've achieved, who've succeeded, who've won." His laugh was much louder now.

The others laughed with him. "What a scene it must have been!" he continued. "They would have been called to an urgent meeting in the boardroom of the museum," he said, waving his large eloquent arms. "Behind and all around them are magnificent portraits of former directors, painted by the leading portrait artists in Greece. Surrounded by these paintings, the board members sit in chairs of equally successful conquerors in commerce and government. Oh, how I hated their success!" he said suddenly, his face turning ugly.

He recovered, wiped his gleaming face with his sleeve, and went on. "They would have wondered why they'd been called—but would have no idea of the real reason. They would have been completely unsuspecting of the catastrophe about to engulf them! They'd sit down, chat for a moment, then turn to the chairman and wait for his words."

The gray steel walls surrounding the small compartment of the sub's captain seemed to expand as Andropous spoke. His eloquent words moved the bulkheads away and replaced them with fine paneled wood and marvelous portrait paintings. His speech turned the steel chairs in which they sat into luxurious boardroom furniture. The shabby, crumpled uniform of the captain, the scruffy jeans and seaman's sweater of the powerful Carlos—these seemed transformed into elegant attire in the refined glow that Andropous's oratory brought into the cabin.

Carlos and the captain could imagine themselves in the elegant suits worn by the important men Andropous described. They were lifted to another world as he spoke, and they pictured themselves among the successful men, the achievers, he portrayed.

Then, the news! The words falling like lightning from Mount Olympus: "The treasures have been stolen! The barrels on the ship are filled with bricks!"

Andropous stood, spreading wide his great arms, lifting his magnificent head as he sketched for Carlos and Captain Stokowski the glorious scene. "Thunderbolts! Lightning! Bombs and missiles sent to destroy mortals below! Oh, what a catastrophe! Their proud, rich faces, red with good food and fine wine, turn ashen gray. Their hard, steely expressions turn slack with shock. Their commanding eyes fill with horror. *They've failed! They've lost! And I've won!*" Andropous finished with a shout of triumph.

Carlos and the captain laughed uproariously at the scene of sudden, utter reversal. From victory to defeat! From success to failure!

"This is what we've done, gentlemen!" Andropous said, his voice quieter now, his caution reminding him to share credit with the men who'd made it possible for his scheme to succeed. "We've hit the capitalists where it hurts the most: we've taken their treasures! We've done it—you and I and our men."

The victors sat back in wonder at what they'd accomplished. Then they thought of the faces of the directors when they heard the news that the treasures had been swapped—for bricks! They roared with laughter again, and again, and again.

There was a timid knock on the cabin door.

Andropous Lycenus didn't hear it. "Think, gentlemen, of their faces! Think how they looked when they heard that they'd been duped! That someone had swapped bricks for the treasures! Oh, it hurts to laugh so much!"

He couldn't contain himself. He laughed and laughed, holding his head in his hands, his shoulders shaking with uncontrollable mirth.

Finally, he looked up, eyes streaming with tears from his laughter. "Gentlemen, we did it!" he repeated. "We beat them!"

There was another knock on the cabin door, bolder this time.

"And to think," Andropous continued, wiping the tears from his eyes with the sleeve of his black turtleneck sweater, "to think that the barrels they thought held treasures of silver and gold were filled with—*bricks*! Bricks!" he repeated, louder this time. "Bricks! Bricks! Bricks!" he roared.

"A toast to bricks!" Carlos shouted, raising his glass on high. Andropous and the captain raised theirs also and joined in the arrogant chorus.

Now they all heard the fist pounding the cabin door. Andropous, Carlos, and Stokowski, thinking they were victors in this fight for communism, turned their flushed, confident faces toward the door. The captain called, "Come in! Come in and show us what we've won!"

The two Greek seamen came slowly into the room, their hands empty. Haltingly, they told what they had found in the barrels. Then they stopped and stared—stared at the ashen faces of Andropous, Carlos, and their captain. Never had they seen such strickened expressions.

For a long moment, none of the three men said a word. Andropous, Carlos, and Stokowski simply looked at the sailors in shock. They took in the story the two seamen told them as if they'd gone completely deaf. They sat uncomprehending, stunned; their faces were now slack with shock and disbelief.

Andropous was the first to recover. "Bricks!" he shouted at the top of his voice, leaping to his feet and slamming the leading sailor against the steel door. "Bricks! What do you mean, bricks?"

The two seamen quailed before the suddenly enraged man. His powerful bulk towered above them in the cramped cabin, threatening, terrifying.

"They've got nothing but bricks in 'em, sir," one of the men said.

"Open the other barrels, you fool!" Andropous shouted in his face. "We must have brought one of the wrong barrels by mistake. Open the others!" He clutched the seaman's jersey and shook him as if he were a limp rag.

"We did that, sir," the terrified sailor replied, backing away from the enraged Andropous. "We opened 'em all. The tops are filled with cardboard. But underneath that, they've all got bricks, all of 'em, all the way to the bottom of the barrels. That's all they've got in 'em—cardboard and bricks. Mostly bricks."

The thick moustache of the seaman twitched nervously as he finished, eyes darting left and right, anywhere but toward the awful faces of the three men.

Then pandemonium reigned in the cabin! The three men exploded! Andropous, Carlos, and Captain Stokowski all shouted at once, yelling their disbelief at the two cowering sailors, ordering them to show the barrels.

The sailors rushed down the narrow steel passage to the forward torpedo room, with the shocked and enraged men stampeding behind them. The frenzied crowd burst into the storage compartment of the old submarine.

There, in the room that had once held deadly torpedoes, Andropous, Carlos, and Stokowski saw the end of their dreams in the mounds of cardboard and bricks that littered the floor around twelve open barrels.

No one said anything at first. The two sailors didn't dare. The three conspirators weren't able. Time stood still.

The captain was the first to come to his senses. "We'll catch that galley!" he shouted. Turning, he stumbled back down the passageway to the control room of the sub. Bursting through the port, he rushed to the executive officer. "Take her up!"

"Up?" the startled officer asked in surprise. He knew that their orders directed them to proceed submerged.

"Up! Up! Up! What do you think I said?" shouted

Stokowski, jamming his face against that of the startled
officer.

"Yes, sir!" the officer replied, quailing before his captain.
What had happened to enrage the man like this? Five minutes before he'd been hilariously happy.

Whirling, Captain Stokowski called to Carlos, who'd just
followed him into the control room. "What was the course
of the galley when you left the ship?"

Carlos struggled to collect his thoughts through the fog
of the wine. Finally he remembered, "One hundred fifteen
degrees."

The captain whirled toward the navigator at his small
desk. "Plot a course to intercept that galley. Assume it's been
traveling at eight knots on that course since the catamaran
left it. Get the skipper of the catamaran and find out the exact
time he left the galley."

He staggered away and leaned against a stack of instruments, holding his throbbing head in his hands. "Call the
cook. Bring us hot tea!"

"Yes, sir."

Andropous stumbled into the control room, struggling to
collect his shattered thoughts and broken dreams. As he
listened to the captain's crisp orders, his dulled eyes showed
no hope whatever.

"What are you doing, captian?" he asked feebly, leaning
weakly against the steel wall, all the arrogance and drive
gone. He was a broken man.

"I'm going to intercept that galley!" the captain said.
"Then I'll send a boarding party over to find the right

barrels and bring them on board. And then I'll sink that galley and everyone on board. We're not quitting now—not when we're so close to success!"

Carlos staggered to a stool beside the navigator and collapsed on it. "But we can't surface, can we? Won't we be spotted by somebody?"

"Who cares now?" the captain asked. "What good does it do us to hide underwater if we don't have what we came to get? We'll submerge again when we've got the right barrels. I'm not quitting!"

The sub was rising to the surface now. The captain let the exec handle the maneuver. In a moment, a seaman came with a tray containing a thermos and several steaming mugs. The captain seized one and motioned the sailor over to Carlos, who took one also. Andropous waved the seaman away and put his head in his hands.

The navigator came to the captain, clipboard in hand. "Sir, this is the course of the galley when the catamaran left her. Then the catamaran steered a course of 180 degrees for 30 minutes to meet us. We're steering 165 degrees—to stay away from the galley's path—as you ordered."

The captain put down the mug of tea he'd been drinking and focused his bloodshot eyes on the chart his navigator was showing him. He studied the lines the navigator had drawn.

"That's where the galley should be now," the navigator continued, "assuming it maintained the speed that Carlos set for it. If we take this course," he pointed to the line he'd drawn on the chart, "we should intercept them here. We can use our surface radar to find them. They can't get away."

"Excellent!" the captain said, slapping his fist into his hand. He spoke then to his executive officer. "Cancel the previous change of course. We'll follow this one. Call the bosun. Have him prepare a boarding party. Get Carlos to explain the layout of the cargo in that galley. Make a map, in fact. We want to know where to go when we board. We've got to be fast!"

He turned to the compass on the wall and studied it for a moment. "It's not too late! We can still get that treasure!"

Carlos spoke, "This time, Captain, I want to open those barrels before we take them on board. We don't want to make this mistake again!"

"You're right!" the captain agreed. "Brief the bosun and his men. Then we must get that cargo aboard as fast as we can. We can't stay on the surface or we'll be found."

Stokowski turned then and leaned against the instrument panel that jutted from the ship's side into the control room. Carlos was struggling to recover his wits; he'd downed as much of the scalding tea as the captain had. He too meant to retrieve this defeat, to bring victory out of it.

But Andropous—the great man, the visionary, the genius who'd planned it all, the orator—had collapsed! Slumped in abject defeat against the navigator's desk, his eyes were hollow, his jaw slack, his will and resolve gone.

The captain thought, not for the first time, of the differences in men. Some have brains, gifts, and all the advantages these bring. But, facing defeat, they collapse. Others, like Carlos, possessed less personal magnetism and gifts, but had more grit. *Courage makes things happen,* Stokowski thought, *just the determination to see something through to a finish. Carlos has that determination. Andropous doesn't.*

Stokowski had it. He meant to recover those treasures. He meant to win. He called for another mug of scalding tea.

CHAPTER 14

"THEY CAN'T GET AWAY FROM US NOW!"

The two big Tomcats roared down from the sky toward the spot where the electronics officer had seen the catamaran and the submarine on his radarscope. The fighters swept around in a huge circle, sensors searching the sea.

"There's nothing there, Charlie," Bob said from the back of the cockpit. "No catamaran, no sub—they're gone."

"What happened?" Charlie demanded, eyes scanning the instrument panel as he led the two planes in a circular search at low altitude. "What worries me is the catamaran. What happened to it? Did the sub sink it and then get away?"

"There's another boat headed west," Bob said, "and about an hour ago it was right beside the catamaran. I spotted them side by side. Then the catamaran ran off while the other stayed on course. We're approaching it now."

"Let's look at it," Charlie said, frustrated by this whole

107

business. "Tell me again why you're sure it was a catamaran."

"It didn't emit any electronic signals from an engine, but it moved too fast for an ordinary sailboat. Only a catamaran can go that fast without engines."

"There's the boat!" Bob said as the two planes flashed by. The lights of the vessel were visible on the sea to their left. "Let's go back around."

"Right," Charlie said. He turned the F-14 in a tight turn and headed back so as to pass close beside the ship.

A flare shot up in the black sky before the approaching Tomcat; then another; then a third!

"They're signaling!" Charlie said. He swept around again in a circle as tight as the big plane could manage at such slow speed and low altitude. Now they'd learn something.

"They're flashing SOS!" Bob said. "They're repeating it over and over."

"Tell the ship," Charlie said. Bob radioed the carrier and reported what they had found. The two planes continued to sweep around the galley in wide circles.

A minute later Bob told his pilot: "The admiral's sending help! I'll signal the boat. Then we can go back to our patrol." Fighter crews hated such low-level flying, especially at night. There was no room to maneuver, no reserve of altitude. Such flying was exacting in the extreme, and they'd be glad when they could climb back five miles into the sky!

On the galley below, Penny had been the first to hear the fighters. "There's a plane!" she cried suddenly.

Then the boys heard it, too. "I think it's coming from our right," Mark said.

"Fire off those flares!" David said at once. "This is our chance!"

Then the two big planes roared by with tremendous noise, their winglights and taillights flashing, flames from their exhaust marking their paths as they swept by.

"Maybe those are navy fighters!" David said excitedly.

"But they've gone!" Penny cried as the planes zoomed away into the night.

Sick at heart, the three watched the dark void into which their hopes for help had disappeared. "Maybe they'll come back," Mark suggested.

Then they heard the planes again.

"Get ready to fire, Mark!" David said.

Mark stepped to the railing, lurched against it with a sudden roll of the ship, recovered his balance, and set off three flares as fast as he could open and fire them. The brilliant lights burst into the sky above the racing galley. Roaring like trains in a rock canyon, the aircraft swept by again.

"They had to see those!" Penny cried. "Now someone will come help us!"

"How will I tell them this whole complicated story?" Mark asked.

"Just signal SOS," David said. "That's all they need to know. Someone's got to find us—before that Russian sub does!"

As the planes came by again, Mark aimed the big light at them and began to signal in Morse code. The fighters swept by, flashing their own lights on and off.

"Those *are* navy fighters!" David cried. "I could see that in the light of the flares!"

"They're acknowledging!" Mark shouted in the noise of the passing Tomcats. "They got the SOS! That's all they need."

The aircraft zoomed by, then climbed for the sky, their exhausts flaming behind the twin engines of each fighter.

"Oh, someone's found us!" Penny cried, throwing her arms around David's neck and bursting into tears. He hugged her with his left arm as his right hand held the ship's wheel. Mark came and pounded David's back.

"Now they'll send help!" he cried jubilantly.

It was then that they realized how terribly alone they had felt. Mr. Spirodes and the two crewmen lay drugged in their bunks below. The Russian sub lurked somewhere in the sea behind them. The galley was steering into the blackness of the night guided only by the compass and the guesses of rank amateurs. But now the U.S. Navy knew where they were. Now they had help!

The wind had changed direction. It was colder now. Spray from the waves began to hit them more often, soaking their clothes. The blackness into which they steered seemed blacker still—but they no longer felt alone!

"Boy, what a difference it makes, knowing the U.S. Navy knows we need help!" David said gratefully.

"And they know where we are!" Penny added.

"Well, it won't be long now," Mark said, stepping to Penny's left again, and putting his strong arm around her waist. "I wonder if they'll send a ship first or a helicopter?"

Far away in the blackness of the night the navy battle group steamed in close formation. On the bridge of the aircraft carrier *Nimitz,* the officer of the deck had called the captain to the bridge. Showing them the position of the galley on the vertical plastic screen, and its direction from the carrier, he explained the message from the fighters.

"It's a ship, sir, flashing SOS signals. We can't make radio contact."

"It's 90 miles away," the captain said, studying the relative positions on the screen before him. "A frigate would need over three hours to reach it. Was it sinking?"

"I don't think so, sir. The fighters said it was going about 14 knots. But one sailboat disappeared from their screen."

"Then they're sure this one's not sinking," the captain said. "Maybe it needs medical help."

He toured the bridge, noting the position of the other ships on the screen. Then he made up his mind. "Detach the trailing frigate. Give them the information. Tell them to rush toward that boat and send a medic by helicopter as soon as they can."

A few minutes later, the frigate trailing the battle group wheeled to its left in a graceful curve and headed toward the reported position of the galley. Inside the bridge, men were plotting the relative position of the two ships, planning the point of interception.

"Call the helicopter crew," the captain of the frigate commanded. "Get a medic ready." He turned back to the officer of the deck. "Estimate the time to launch. We don't want the chopper to take off too soon and not have enough fuel to hang around that boat."

"Yes, sir."

"Tell sonar to keep a watch for that sub the plane reported."

On the bridge of the *Nimitz*, the carrier's captain was pondering the significance of the fighter's report concerning the submarine and the disappearing sailboat. The more he thought of it, the more he thought this could be a factor in the SOS the fighters had seen from the other boat. He called his executive officer.

More than 120 miles east and south of the *Nimitz*, the Russian submarine was on the surface, making top speed. The sub's surface radar was scanning the sea like a bird dog sniffing its prey. The bridge of the long conning tower was jammed with extra lookouts. The captain and Carlos moved among them.

"What are our chances, Captain?" Carlos yelled into the wind. That cold blast and the hot tea had brought clarity to his befuddled brain.

"Excellent!" the captain yelled back. "We know their course. We'll catch them soon."

"What if they change course?" Carlos asked. "The crew's drugged, but if something should go wrong and the boat changes direction, can we still find them?"

"We can. We'll head for the position we plotted. That's the maximum distance they could reach at the speed they were going. If they're not there, we'll just follow that course back until we find them. They can't go fast enough to escape," he said confidently.

He went over the tactical situation in his mind and could see no flaws in his plan. "The galley can't get away from us now!"

To the west of the submarine, heading directly away from their expected course, the galley labored in increasingly heavy seas. The wind was stronger now, blowing the spray over the side of the ship.

Penny had gone below to find jackets and hats, and brought these to the two boys. Then she went to the galley's kitchen and made more hot tea. She struggled bringing it up the steps to the deck and then to the quarterdeck. But the boys drank it gratefully.

Then David had an idea. "I think we should be keeping a lookout with binoculars. We'd have a hard time seeing something directly in front of us because of those masts and the prow.

"Good idea," Mark agreed. "But let me take the wheel and give you a break."

They swapped places. David picked up the binoculars and went forward.

Mark had an idea. "Penny, why don't you go below to Mr. Spirodes's cabin and get his binoculars. One of us should be watching to the rear. We don't want to be surprised or run down!"

At the prow of the galley, David began scanning the dark

sea ahead and to each side of the galley as it sliced through the dark waters. Penny, at the stern, looked behind them and also to each side. Mark held the wheel in the difficult seas, struggling to keep the ship on the course indicated by the compass. The dark enveloped them with oppressive force while the cold wind chilled them steadily. They stamped on the deck and flailed their arms to keep warm.

"What'll we do if we see the submarine behind us, Mark?" Penny asked in a voice that was calmer than her thoughts.

"Fire off all the flares we have," he replied instantly. He'd been thinking about that. "There's a whole pack of them in that closet behind me. Could you get them ready?"

"I don't know how to fire them," she said as she got the flares out and stacked them on the deck by the wheel.

"I do," he said. "I'm an expert. I'll show you how!" he laughed.

She hugged him for trying to keep them both cheered.

"I don't think we'll see that sub again," he said. "But if it does come up behind us, I'll give you the wheel, then fire those flares at it. Someone's bound to see all the fireworks." He knew that someone *could.* The question was, *would* they?

"Actually," he added, "there won't be any need. Those navy fighters saw our SOS and they signaled to us that they understood. They've already radioed their ship for help, and help is probably already on the way. Penny, keep your eyes open! Run tell David to do the same. Take him a couple of these flares. We've got to fire one as soon as we hear them coming."

Mark was exuberant as he thought of the battle group's resources. Why, they'd send a helicopter long before that sub could reach them! If, that is, the sub was really looking for them. He doubted that it was.

Penny picked up several flares and went down the steps to the deck, then walked quickly along to the foredeck, holding to the rail. Spray from the waves below was reaching the deck now, and she felt the saltwater on her face as she walked. Reaching the steps to the foredeck, she climbed these, and joined David at the bow.

"Hi!" she said, coming close so they could talk. The wind was strong at the bow of the ship.

"Hey, there!" he replied, delighted at her company.

"Mark says you should be looking for a plane or probably a helicopter from the battle group. They'll be coming any time now, he thinks. Here are some flares for you to use when you see them. We don't want them to miss us." She handed him the flares she'd brought.

"Great!" he said. "Boy, will I be glad to see a helicopter!"

"Me, too," she replied. "But why do you and Mark think that's what they'll send?"

"Well, the fighter planes that we saw really can't help us. And it would take a ship hours to get here. Only a helicopter could reach us in a hurry. All the navy warships carry helicopters. And we're sure they'll answer our SOS."

"Oh, that's good news!" she replied. "Aren't you cold?" She shivered in the wind that swept across the bow.

"A bit, I guess," he answered. He reached out and put his arm around her. "Thanks for the jacket, though. That makes it bearable."

They stood there in companionable silence as the galley cut through the Aegean Sea and the wind swept across the ship.

After a couple of minutes, Penny said, reluctantly. "I guess I'd better go back. Mark wants me to use the binoculars and keep watch behind us, so no one can sneak up."

"I think he's right," David agreed, equally reluctantly.

"I'm sure the navy will be here soon!" she said. "Watch for them!"

"I will," he promised. "Be careful going back along that deck; the seas are rough now. Hold the rail."

"O.K.," she said, lingering a moment. Even though they stood close together, they could barely see each other's faces in the dim light cast by the bow lights. She reached out and touched his cheek lightly with her fingertips, then turned and went carefully down the steps.

David watched her disappear in the darkness. He saw her dimly again as she passed the deck light amidships. Then she was gone. Alone now, he turned and began to search the sky systematically, looking ahead and to each side of the galley as it drove through the dark waters.

CHAPTER 15

"THERE'S THE GALLEY, CARLOS!"

Carlos and the captain were enraged. They'd approached the point of interception as they'd plotted, but their instruments gave no indication of a boat ahead. The two men had tumbled below to consult the navigator. Hurriedly they'd examined the alternatives.

"They should be here, Captain," the navigator insisted.

"They should be," Captain Stokowski agreed, "but they're not. We've got to think."

"Captain," Carlos said, "Mr. Spirodes and the crew were drugged. Those American kids were asleep in their cabins. Either the ship's automatic steering gear came loose and the ship changed course, or those kids got out and steered a different direction." He was in a towering rage at his carelessness in counting on those kids to sleep. He should have drugged their food, too!

"If the steering gear came loose, the galley won't be far from the course it was on," Stokowski said. "If those kids are steering it, it could be anywhere. But not far! It just can't

117

go that fast."

"Reverse course," he commanded.

Turning back to the chart on the navigator's table, he resumed his speculations. "If the kids did wake up and take over the ship, which way would they steer?" he asked.

Carlos replied at once. "I think they'd reverse course and go back the way they came. They know that they don't know these seas. They'd go a way they thought was safe. They'd just reverse course."

Carlos continued. "I've been thinking, Captain. We've got to ask if there's a connection between the barrels we've got and the disappearance of the galley."

"What do you mean?" Stokowski asked.

"I *know* where those barrels of art were stored because I put them there," Carlos said emphatically. "Someone moved them! Other barrels were swapped for the ones I loaded."

"Who did the swapping?" the captain asked.

"Probably Mr. Spirodes," Carlos answered thoughtfully. "Somehow he found out about the treasures and swapped them. But when could he have done that? We drugged his coffee and he went to sleep after supper."

"Maybe he did find out about the art," Stokowski said, "and ordered someone to swap the barrels when you were asleep."

"But his crewmen were drugged," Carlos said. Then his eyes widened. "Those American teenagers! No one else could have been awake while Andropous and I slept, because we drugged all the others. Only those kids could have done it! They're the ones who moved those barrels and replaced them with the ones carrying bricks. And they must have changed the galley's course to get away from us!" He stood up in a fury, finding it inconceivable that this brilliant plan had been thwarted by three American teenagers.

"Well, it won't do them any good," the captain said decisively. "They're not going to get away from us now. We'll catch that galley, we'll get those barrels with the art, and we'll sink the ship and everyone on board. We can't let anyone survive to tell what happened." His face was grim. There was no mistaking his determination. There would be no survivors to tell what had become of the stolen art.

Almost 100 miles west of the submarine, the frigate prepared to launch its helicopter. Pilot and copilot had taken their places in the craft's cabin. Behind them sat two medics with their emergency medical gear. They were ready to go. The pilot started the engine and the giant blades began to whirl. Then, without warning, the lights went out in the helicopter's cabin.

The message reached the ship's bridge at once. "They're having problems with the helicopter, Captain."

"What kind of problems?" the captain demanded instantly. They couldn't afford problems now. The helicopter *had* to take off and reach that ship! Lives might be in danger on that boat, and they had to launch at once.

The sailor spoke again. "They say the chopper's lights went off, sir."

On the stern of the frigate the helicopter was surrounded

by crewmen. Angrily, the pilot jumped to the deck, helmet in hand, and strode to the hangar, followed by the copilot and the two medics. Repairmen climbed into the craft and began work in the cabin. The pilot called the bridge and asked to speak to the ship's captain.

"Sir, they say it may take them an hour to fix it," he said.

The captain's face was grim. An hour to fix the helicopter! Maybe more. Then an 80-mile flight to the boat that had flashed its SOS to the fighters. No telling how long the chopper would have to search for the target once it got to the reported area.

Frustrated at the delay, the captain turned and strode to the other side of the bridge. This was terrible. It could take two hours to land medics on that boat!

To the east, the Golf-II submarine plowed through the choppy waters of the eastern Mediterranean in hot pursuit of the fleeing galley. "We should see them in an hour and three quarters, Captain," the navigator said. He'd been studying his chart again, plotting their course, the suspected course of the galley, and the relative speeds of the two ships.

"Good!" Captain Stokowski said, slapping his palm with his fist. "They can't radio for help because Carlos smashed their equipment."

He turned and told the officer on deck to check on the boarding crew. Then he climbed up the ladder to the open bridge and joined Carlos and the lookouts. "Maybe an hour and three quarters, the navigator says."

"Excellent!" Carlos replied. He'd been going over in his mind their plan to board the galley. With the crew still drugged in their cabins, the three teenagers wouldn't have a chance of stopping a boarding party. Carlos and his men would storm the boat, check the barrels below, bring up the ones with the treasures, transfer them to the sub, and then sink the galley and everyone on board.

"Listen, Captain," he said, "we put red ropes around the tops of the barrels with the Greek treasures. And I loaded them on the starboard side of the cargo hold in two rows. Those are the barrels we took—ones with red ropes on 'em. Mr. Spirodes got someone to swap the barrels with others in the hold, and then to put the red lines on the barrels of ballast. That was no accident; they really tried to fool us."

"And they did!" the captain said grimly. "But they'll pay—*with their lives!*"

"They will. But I believe the barrels we want are just across from the ones we took; that'd be the easiest way to make the swap. They didn't have much time. So we'll check those first. We can rip off the tops in a second, and get to the false bottoms. We know that the treasures are under them."

"Brief the boarding party, will you, Carlos?" Captain Stokowski said. "The more they know before they board the galley, the quicker we'll be able to get the barrels and submerge."

"Right," Carlos said. He went down the ladder.

Below, Andropous Lycenus still sat slumped in his chair. His eyes were closed, his head propped against the steel wall. *His spirit's broken*, Carlos thought sadly. Carlos passed his brother and headed for the torpedo room in the forward part of the sub. Here he found the bosun and the boarding crew and briefed them on the situation in the hold of the galley.

Far ahead of the sub in the blackness of the night, the galley carved its way through the increasingly rough waters. David stood in the bow of the ship, scanning the sky with his binoculars, sweeping from left, to dead ahead, to right, then back again. Almost 100 feet behind him, Mark and Penny stood on the quarterdeck. Mark gripped the wheel, straining to keep the ship on course in the choppy seas, watching the compass before him.

Time passed slowly. Minute after agonizing minute went by, with no sound of a plane or helicopter. "Why don't they come, Mark?" Penny asked finally. "Shouldn't they be here by now?"

The wind cut through their clothes, chilling them through.

"I don't know," he replied, trying to keep the anxiety out of his voice. "But they'll come as soon as they can. It shouldn't be long," he said hopefully. He put his arm around her, but then had to grab the wheel again and hold it with both hands as the waves beat against the ship.

"I'd better look behind us," she said, turning away and picking up the binoculars. Leaning her body against the storage locker behind the wheel to steady herself, she began to sweep the seas through the glasses. "It's so dark, Mark," she said in a small voice. "I can't see where the sea leaves off and the sky begins."

"That's O.K.," her brother replied. "That's really what we want. We don't want to see *anything!*"

For another half hour or so the ship plowed its way through the uneven seas. David at the bow and Penny at the stern searched the sea and sky for ships or planes. But they found nothing. Then David came back down the deck to the wheel.

"Time to swap, Mark," he said. "I didn't realize that I'd left you fighting that wheel so long!"

"Well," Mark replied gratefully, "I'm glad for the change! The seas are rough and you've got to wrestle with the thing all the time."

Mark stepped back and let David take his place, grateful for the relief. Now his muscles began to complain. He hadn't realized what a strain the job had been!

"Remember in the book of Esther in the Bible how the Lord delivered the Jews just as Haman's plot was about to get them all killed?" David said. "When everything looked hopeless, they got help and defended themselves."

"Let's keep praying and trusting God to deliver us like He did them," Mark said.

Then he walked slowly to the bow, taking David's place, hoping he'd have the chance to fire flares at an approaching helicopter. David and Penny stood at the wheel, huddled together in the wind, praying. But they heard nothing.

Another half hour went by. Mark came back and relieved David at the wheel. David went forward again, to watch for rescuing navy ships or helicopters. He saw nothing. Another half hour passed.

Crashing through the dark seas behind the galley, the sub came in range of its surface radar. The operator called the bridge. "We've got a contact."

"It won't be long, Carlos!" Captain Stokowski said.

Swiftly the submarine closed the distance to the galley. The boarding party went over the diagram of the galley that Carlos had drawn. On the open bridge of the conning tower, extra lookouts joined the men already searching for their prey. The tension in the ship increased as the crew realized they had almost caught their target. Time passed swiftly now.

Suddenly a lookout yelled, "Ship ahead!"

Stokowski ran up the ladder, raised his binoculars, and looked in the direction the sailor pointed. Then he yelled for Carlos to join him.

Carlos raced up the ladder of the conning tower and wedged himself among the captain and the lookouts. He peered through the blackness of the night, but without the aid of binoculars he couldn't see what the others had found. "There's the galley, Carlos!" Stokowski cried back. "We've caught them!"

CHAPTER 16

"BOARD THE GALLEY!"

Get the boarders ready!" Captain Stokowski shouted.

The message was passed down to the torpedo room where Carlos and the bosun were drilling the boarding crew on the layout of the galley's cargo area.

"Let's go!" the bosun said. "Every man get a pistol. First we'll secure the wheel and steering of the ship. Then you six will follow Carlos to the cargo room, locate the barrels we want, and start bringing them up."

The men moved through the narrow passage of the submarine toward the control room. They were ready. They knew their job.

Topside, the captain was shouting orders. "Bring the other lookouts! We've got to keep a sharp watch for planes. Our surface radar will spot ships, but we don't have any aircraft warning radar. We'll have to rely on our eyes." He cursed the shortsightedness of the people in the dockyard who'd stripped his sub of such vital equipment.

Men clambered to their posts on the long bridge structure

125

of the Golf-II sub as the ship closed on the galley.

"Mark!" Penny cried, leaning against the rail at the stern of the fleeing galley. "There's something behind us!" She strained to see through the heavy binoculars, but the dark of the night sky and sea made it very difficult.

"What is it?" Mark asked, distressed.

"It's a dark shape, and it's following us," she said, her heart sinking.

"Get David!" Mark said urgently. "Tell him to bring his flares! Hurry!"

Penny ran to the steps, went down quickly, and raced the length of the deck to the foredeck. Running up those steps she called, "David! A ship is coming behind us! Bring the flares!"

His heart sinking at the realization that they'd lost the race for safety, David picked up the pile of flares from the deck and raced after Penny. He ran up the steps to join Mark and Penny at the wheel.

"There it is," Penny said, pointing.

"Wow, it's coming fast!" David said.

"We'd better fire off as many flares as we can," Mark said grimly. "Somebody's got to see them."

"Go ahead, Mark," David said urgently. "I'll steer."

On the bridge of the USS *Nimitz*, Captain MacLean waited anxiously for news from the frigate. The frigate's captain had radioed that his helicopter was being repaired. Captain MacLean was waiting to hear that the job was done and that medics were on the way to the boat that had signaled for help.

Twenty minutes passed, and no message arrived from the frigate. Then 20 more. Suddenly a signalman interrupted Captain MacLean's troubled thoughts. "Message from the frigate, Captain. The chopper's on the way."

"Acknowledge!" the captain said, stepping to the plastic board where the tactical situation was displayed. Now he was wondering to himself how long it would take them to reach that boat. "Let me talk to the F-14s on patrol," he commanded.

"Aye, Captain." A moment later the signalman said, "I've got the flight leader, sir."

"What's his name?" the captain inquired.

"Charlie McBride, sir."

The captain spoke into the radio speaker before him. "Charlie, this is the skipper. Where are you and what can you see?"

"Sir, we're at 20,000 feet, 15 miles east and south of the ship. The sub we spotted some time ago surfaced again and headed for an interception point with the ship that signaled us for help. They would have intercepted if the boat had stayed on course. But it reversed its course when the other boat left to rendezvous with the sub. It's been going twice as fast as it was; looks like it's running for its life!"

A sailor handed the captain a mug of coffee as Charlie continued. "The sub is closing fast, sir, on the surface."

The captain took this in. "You reported earlier that your electronics officer thought the boat that disappeared was a catamaran."

"Yes, sir. Our instruments couldn't pick up any engine signature, but it moved too fast for an ordinary sailboat. He's sure it was a catamaran."

The captain thought about the disappearing boat for a moment. "Do you think the sub sank it, Charlie?"

"That's what we figure, Captain. Now the sub's almost caught the boat that flashed us the SOS."

Captain MacLean made up his mind. "Go take a look, Charlie."

"Yes, sir!" the fighter pilot said eagerly.

"Watch out for that chopper from the frigate. It's going to land medics on the galley."

"Yes, sir." Instantly the two planes swept through the dark night in a graceful curve and aimed like arrows toward the galley far below.

On the sea, the menacing dark shape of the submarine sliced through the choppy seas, overtaking the galley rapidly. A signalman in the conning tower began to flash signals in international Morse code, ordering the sailing ship to heave to.

Turning to Captain Stokowski beside him, the signalman said, "They won't acknowledge."

"Keep signaling. I want them to know why we're going to sink them when we're through!" the captain replied grimly.

"Aye, Captain."

On board the fleeing galley, there was only one thing the three Americans could do to delay their capture.

"Fire the flares, Mark!" David yelled.

Mark fired one of the flares, aiming it high, lobbing it above and in front of the approaching sub. Even as the flare climbed into the air, he fired another, this one slightly to his left.

The first flare burst with a dazzling flash above the pursuing ship, sending flashes of pure light in every direction. Then the second flare exploded above and to the right of the sub, bathing it in intense light, blinding the men on deck.

Mark ran to the other side of the galley and fired a flare up and out to the side. "I'll spread these out," he yelled. "Someone's *got* to see them!"

The brilliant lights flamed in the dark sky, illuminating all beneath them, then falling slowly to the sea below.

David struggled with the wheel as the galley raced at top speed into the choppy waves. Penny, beside him, stared at the deadly approaching submarine through the binoculars.

"David," she said, "there are a lot of men on the front of the submarine."

David glanced quickly behind and saw the sub in the light of the descending flares. *It's just 300 yards away*, he thought, *and closing fast*. High waves curled up from either side of the bow as the warship crashed through the waters.

"Fire some at the sub, Mark," David yelled. "Maybe it'll blind their night vision."

Mark fired at the sub. Bright light again bathed the dark vessel. Then he ran back to the quarterdeck and thrust some flares into Penny's hand. "Help me, Penny! Watch how I do it."

Both of them now fired flares at the sub, just over its bow and conning tower, bathing the ship and the men above deck with blinding light. Mark and Penny were opening and firing flares as fast as they could now.

The men on the deck and conning tower were yelling with rage, covering their faces with their arms, and cursing the light that blinded their vision.

"Slow the ship!" the captain roared. "We can't hit that boat!" He turned and shouted into the speaker tube to the helmsman below. "They're blinding us with flares up here. Watch the scope!"

"Yes, sir!"

"How will we board without smashing that galley?" the exec asked. "We can't see!"

"Wait a minute!" Stokowski replied grimly. "Soon we'll be too close for those flares to bother us. They'll burst behind. Now we've got them!"

On board the struggling galley, David had a desperate idea. He shouted to Mark and Penny. "I'll turn and try to ram!" Wrenching the wheel with all his strength, he put the boat into a sharp turn. At the same time, he flipped the control switch that put the port engine into reverse. Quickly the galley changed course, turning south, into the wind, then east, spinning almost as quickly as if 200 rowers had turned it around in battle.

The wind heeled the ship over as it turned, plunging the edge of the deck under the water. The wooden railing on the side splintered under the force of tons of seawater that crashed aboard. The galley turned faster now. Soon its deadly bow pointed directly at the rapidly approaching sub.

"They're turning, Captain!" the exec yelled. "They must be surrendering!"

"Excellent!" Stokowski replied, a triumphant smile wreathing his face. "They'd better." Men began to relax on the submarine.

"But those flares are still going up!" Carlos yelled over the wind.

"Probably a crewman who didn't get the message to surrender," the captain said. "They've given up. We've got them now. Head to the right," he ordered. "We'll stop beside them, tie on, and board."

Rapidly the two ships closed, bows aimed each at the other.

Two miles above and closing fast, the pilots of the big twin-engine fighters saw the explosion of flares in the darkness below.

"What's going on down there?" Charlie asked his wingman, as the sea below was lit by bursts of incandescent light.

From the backseat, Bob answered his question. "The sub's almost got 'em, Charlie. They may want help, but they sure don't want it from that sub! I guess they're hoping someone will see the flares and come to their rescue. Those lights will sure blind the men on the sub's bridge for a while."

Charlie spoke to his wingman. "Jerry, drop back. I'm going to go low over the bow of that sub. You follow me and do the same."

"Bob," Charlie said to his electronics man in the back-seat. "Call the ship and tell the captain what's going on."

On the galley below, David, Mark, and Penny knew that the game was almost up. "They're getting too close for the flares," Mark said.

"I know," David replied. "All I can do now is aim the galley at them. Maybe the ram will put a hole in their hull. There's nothing else to do. When we get close, you better hold on to the rail!"

"Watch that boat!" the sub's captain yelled again. "Don't let us crash into it!"

"Don't worry, Captain," his exec replied. "We're slowing down. They can't get away."

"They can't!" the enraged captain yelled. "But those flares could call help from 50 miles away! We've got to come alongside and stop them!"

"They're aimed right at us, Captain!" a lookout yelled. "We're going to hit!"

"Aircraft! Aircraft!" another lookout screamed, just seconds before the night was shattered by the roaring of the F-14's twin engines as it flashed across the bow of the sub-marine. The boarders on the bow of the sub were staggered by the explosion of the plane's sonic boom.

Screaming with shocked surprise, the captain and lookouts struggled to make sense of the dangerous flyby. All eyes strained to the right of the ship, trying desperately to identify the flashing fighter that had just gone over. No one saw the second Tomcat approach.

Another flash of wing lights and engine exhaust and another terrible sonic boom struck the men on the sub's bridge and deck. The boarding party tumbled frantically back to the open port of the conning tower and scrambled desperately inside. Here they crouched, cowering behind the thin metal side of the ship.

"They're going to ram us!" a lookout shouted.

Shocked, the captain and crew turned their heads back just in time to see the fast-approaching galley—aimed straight at them!

Then David threw the engines into reverse, slowing the speed of the galley. It had almost stopped when its ram plowed into the thin hull of the ballast tank on the submarine's side. Seawater began to pour into the punctured compartment. The galley shuddered to a stop as the submarine passed across its bow from right to left. Several men had fallen from the sub's deck into the rough seas from the force of the galley's blow.

"Hard right!" the captain yelled, shocked at the sudden collision. Carlos cursed as the galley slid by, knowing better than the sub's captain what the galley had just done to them.

"They rammed you, Captain!" he yelled frantically. "They've punctured your hull! Back away!"

The captain shook his fist in helpless rage at the dark sky and the unseen fighters that had zoomed so low across his bow. He cursed the fools in the navy dockyard that had stripped his ship of weapons and the vital radar that would warn of approaching aircraft.

"Check for damage below!" he yelled into the speaking tube to the officer below. "Call the damage control party. We've been rammed! So close we were!" he shouted bitterly. "So close!"

"Captain," a lookout said, pointing to their left, "they're coming again!"

Screaming vengefully from the sky at 1,000 miles an hour, the big fighters roared toward the damaged submarine.

Ninety miles away Captain MacLean gave the order to the fighter pilots to escalate the warning. "Fire across their bow if they don't stop, Charlie," he said into the radio.

"*Yes, sir!*" the delighted pilot replied. Already in a fast low dive, he aimed, through the scope before him. The sub was so close to the galley! A few dozen 20-millimeter shells in the water in front of the sub should help the skipper come to his senses. Charlie squeezed the trigger.

Over 100 shells shot from the big gun on the left side of the Tomcat's fuselage. Sailors on the sub saw a terrifying streak of tracers arching toward them out of the night. Men were shouting wildly, ducking behind the steel shell of the conning tower.

"Take her down! Take her down!" the captain yelled. Men tumbled frantically down the steel ladders of the sub, into the hull. The ocean in front of them exploded in a marching line of water flung high by the shells of the strafing Tomcat. Another sonic boom hammered the ears of the submariners—and the desperate Americans on the galley.

A mile away, the pilots of the helicopter watched in awe as the flares lit up the night sky. "What do they think this is?" the pilot asked. "The Fourth of July?"

Just then the frigate captain warned him of the diving Tomcats. "Give those fighters lots of room!"

First one and then the second Tomcat flashed low over the submarine.

"The fighters have zoomed the sub, Captain," the helicopter pilot radioed.

Then he saw one of the fighters dive again. "Wow! It's firing across the sub's bow!"

"The sub's turning away!" the copilot yelled.

"You're right," his pilot replied. "Look! Now it's diving, Captain," he said into the radio. "The sub's turning away and it's diving! The fighters have driven it under!"

"Land the medics," the frigate captain commanded.

CHAPTER 17

IN THE HANDS OF A REAL SAILOR!

The crash of the sonic boom over the sub's bow smashed against the galley with terrible force. Stunned, David, Mark, and Penny looked up as the fiery exhaust of the giant twin-engined fighter flashed away into the dark.

"It's the navy! It's the navy fighters!" David yelled.

"Wow!" Mark yelled back. "What a noise!"

"Look at the men on the submarine!" Penny cried, watching again through the binoculars. "They're panicking! Some fell over the side when we hit them!"

Hopping with excitement, she handed the binoculars to her brother.

Then the second F-14 shattered the night sky with another sonic boom, catching them all by surprise once again.

Yelling and waving wildly, the three teens watched the submarine swerve away to their left, illuminated by the still-descending flares.

"They're turning away! They're turning away!" Penny

136

screamed, pointing at the low-lying deadly shape just 50 yards away from the galley. David had thrown both engines into reverse and the galley was moving rapidly away from the sub.

Then the roar of one of the Tomcats' guns, the line of bright tracers, and the rising wall of water just ahead of the submarine piled blow after blow on the battered senses of the three teenagers. Words failed them! They just yelled and yelled with joy and excitement as they watched the black hull with the elongated bridge turn farther and farther away.

"Look!" David shouted, almost hoarse now, "the sub's going under! The fighters have driven it under!"

Already the water covered the ship's deck and slapped against the long conning tower. One of the Tomcats roared by as the waves splashed against the base of the sub's periscopes. Then the sub was gone.

"I hear a helicopter!" Penny shouted, whirling around and staring in the dark sky to their right.

The helicopter's rotors beat a sudden wave of air against the three teens on the quarterdeck, the noise hitting them with surprising force, pounding their already battered hearing. Beside themselves with happiness, voices now hoarse, they could barely shout.

"Watch the lines to the mast of that boat!" the pilot of the chopper yelled as one of the medics hooked on the line that would lower him to the galley and stepped out into the air.

David struggled with the wheel to keep the galley on a straight course as the helicopter slowly came directly overhead, its engine and rotors making a terrific noise. Mark and Penny held to the rail and gazed up at the descending medic, a dark blur in the bright landing light shining directly at them from the swaying helicopter.

"How can he land in this wind?" Penny cried to Mark as the medic's body swirled erratically above them. The boat rose and plunged in the choppy waves, rolling from side to side.

"I don't know!" Mark shouted back, heart in his throat at the man's dangerous descent to the plunging deck.

But the medic was on the deck in an instant. Landing quickly, he stumbled to his feet, released the line, and came toward Mark and Penny. The line snaked back up to the helicopter, hauled in by the winch.

"What's the trouble?" he asked.

They had hardly begun to answer when the second medic stepped out of the plane and began his descent to the plunging deck.

"Well," Mark replied, "the captain and his two crewmen were drugged last night. We can't wake them up."

"Lead me to them!" the medic replied, picking up his pack from the deck.

"Penny," Mark said, "take him below. I'll wait for this next man."

Penny led the medic quickly to the steps, down to the deck, then below to Mr. Spirodes's cabin. Opening the door, she showed him the vessel's skipper. He lay on his bed, unconscious, still wearing the clothes he'd had on the day before.

The other medic was winched down from the helicopter to the deck, and Mark led him below.

The helicopter rose to a safer altitude and flew beside the

galley, waiting for the medics to radio their findings. Five minutes passed, then 10.

"Why don't those men radio and tell us what's going on?" the copilot asked the pilot.

Finally, the medics, jammed into Mr. Spirodes's cabin with Mark and Penny, radioed the chopper on their portable radio. Haltingly, one of the medics told the pilot what the kids had just told him.

The pilot was staggered by the tale. "What are you babbling about?" he asked incredulously into the mike on his helmet. "Have you guys gotten into the ship's rum already?"

Minutes later, the pilot called the frigate. Soon he was speaking to the captain, repeating the message he'd gotten from the medic, wondering if the captain would ground him for mental instability.

"Are those guys crazy?" the captain asked, stunned by the message.

"That's what I thought, sir," the pilot replied, "but they swear that's what those teenagers are telling them. And there are three drugged men on the boat. And there was a submarine chasing them. The medics believe them, Captain. And there's lots of rope lying around the cargo hold where some barrels have been stored. And the radio's been smashed by *somebody*, sir!"

"And they say that they've got the treasures from that Greek museum that all the TV news in the Mediterranean have been talking about? Those things are on board the galley?" the frigate captain asked.

"Yes, sir," the pilot answered firmly, "that's what they say."

The frigate captain knew he had to brief the carrier on what he'd learned so far. How would they receive such a weird story? He sighed. What would this do to his career? "Get me the carrier," he told his exec. In a minute he was speaking to Captain MacLean.

"Well, sir, the men we put on that boat called just a minute ago. They said the only crew remaining on the boat were drugged last night, and are still unconscious. Three American teenagers are sailing the ship, trying to escape that submarine. They told the medic that the other crew members deserted on a catamaran to rendezvous with a Russian submarine—the one that was chasing them. They claim that they've got the stolen Greek treasures on board—you know, it's been on the news all week. I told them to confirm that the treasures are there."

"Report the minute you hear from them," Captain MacLean ordered. He turned and looked bleakly at Admiral Zimmerman, who'd just come to the *Nimitz*'s bridge. "It's wild, admiral," he said, as he sketched in the weird story he'd just heard. "The frigate captain told them to search the rest of the boat's hold. We can't send a message like this without some proof."

"Well," the admiral replied, "that was a Golf-II sub your pilots warned away from that galley. It was up to something." He shook his head in disgust. "This cruise has gone off without a hitch. It's the best training cruise we've had. And to end up with this insane scenario—shooting at a Russian submarine, of all things!"

The frigate captain was radioing again. Captain MacLean

and Admiral Zimmerman turned to the speaker phone. Zimmerman leaned over to speak into it. "We just got this from the helicopter, sir, who got it from the medics on board the galley. They looked in those barrels, Captain, all twelve of them, and . . . ."

Twenty minutes later, after more calls to the frigate and the helicopter, more relayed messages from the medics on the galley, the admiral gave a crisp command. "Put this together in a coherent story and pass it to fleet headquarters. At once!"

Back on the galley, the leading medic, a huge Hawaiian by the name of McPherson, was enjoying himself. He was back on a real boat again! Those men below would sleep off the stuff they'd been given without any help from him. He explored the galley, then joined David on the quarterdeck.

"Why use those engines when you've got real sails? Let's see how this ship *sails!*" he suggested.

Without waiting for a reply, he flipped off the engines, then ran down the deck to ready the sails. Running back and forth, he soon had the galley under both sails, slicing into the choppy seas, headed on her original course to the island of Rhodes.

"I've never sailed a boat like this. What is it?" he cried into the howling wind. David told him about the Greek galleys of ancient times, and how this was an exact replica. The velocity of the wind had dropped, David noticed. The seas weren't as rough as they'd been, either. Everything seemed better with a navy helicopter nearby and two sailors on board!

The Hawaiian took over the wheel and laughed with sheer delight. "Man, I haven't been on a real boat in two years! Just steel boxes!"

Mark, Penny, and the other medic emerged on the deck from the forward hatch and came toward the quarterdeck where the big Hawaiian played the wheel as if the boat were a new toy. They ran up the steps to join David beside McPherson, while the other medic stumbled unsteadily behind them.

"Ben," McPherson yelled to the medic, "call the chopper. Tell them we've got things under control, but we can't leave yet. That we've got to watch these men to make sure they're out of danger."

Ben laughed. "Yeah, and don't tell them you're playing with a boat!"

"Right!" the Hawaiian laughed back. "Don't tell them that!"

"Can I fix you men some eggs and coffee?" Penny asked, stumbling into McPherson as the galley gave a sudden lurch.

"Honey, that's a great idea!" the Hawaiian said, broad face breaking into a grateful smile as he steadied her with his massive arm. He turned the wheel smoothly and the galley came back on course.

"I'll go with you," David told her. They moved carefully across the steeply sloping deck, then down the steps to the kitchen below. The tops of waves were splashing over the ship's rail now, David saw, glancing back. The deck was wet.

"Oh, David," she said, as they entered the vessel's small kitchen, "thank God they came!"

"And thank God those fighters drove away the sub!"
he replied. "They were about to board us."

"But you rammed the submarine, David! You stopped
them from boarding us!" Her eyes shone as she looked up
at him.

On the steeply angled deck above them, Mark yelled to
the Hawaiian at the wheel. "Where'd you learn to sail?"
He was thrilled at the vessel's speed under sail.

"On Maui," the big man grinned. "I grew up in a boat.
Man, I haven't had a wheel in my hand for two years!"

Ben returned from the radio. "I told them we'd have to
stay here a while and watch the drugged men. And that
everything was under control. The chopper will stay alongside in case that sub comes back. They asked if we needed
any more help."

"No!" the Hawaiian replied quickly. "Tell them there's
a master sailor on board and everything is under control."

In Moscow, the badly shaken Admiral Jurginov,
Commander of the Russian Navy, sat at his desk, trying to
reach the Admiral of the Black Sea Fleet. The communi-
cation from the American government that one of Russia's
submarines had stolen the Greek treasures had shaken him
badly. Wires were buzzing with messages back and forth between an outraged Greece, Russia, and the United States. A
major diplomatic storm was brewing—just when Russia was

trying to secure more financial help from the Western nations. The situation appeared to be catastrophic. Jurginov had to recall that submarine before terrible international complications developed!

Finally he lost patience when Admiral Zukhov of the Black Sea Fleet refused to come to the phone. Admiral Jurginov went berserk. "Call naval security," he shouted at his aide. "Have them bring Admiral Zukhov to the phone if they have to drag him in chains!" He slammed the phone down and looked wildly around the room.

"Something's wrong!" he said to his flag lieutenant who'd just rushed into the room. "Call Zukhov's second-in-command. Tell him I am taking command of the Black Sea Fleet until we settle this. Alert all the staffs. Call everyone to headquarters."

"Yes, sir."

"And get me the commander of the air wing under Zukhov's command. I want to know what planes we have that could reach that sub in a hurry. We may have to sink it ourselves—before it starts a war!"

He thought of something else. "Signal the sub right away. We can't wait to go through the chain of command now. Order the sub to ignore all previous instructions, to cease all operations, and to contact me at once and to take orders only from me."

"Yes, sir." The visibly disturbed man rushed from the room.

Admiral Jurginov put his head in his hands. He *had* to bring that sub back before the Americans or the Greeks felt compelled to sink it! But where was the admiral in command of the Black Sea Fleet? What was going on?

Admiral Zimmerman on the *Nimitz* was in contact with his fleet commander. "Sir, we've got a helicopter alongside that galley. We've landed two medics on board. They're attending the skipper and his crew, who were heavily drugged by the thieves who stole their cargo and escaped on the catamaran. I've got two antisubmarine planes on the way to the galley, with fighter cover, to ward off that Russian sub if it returns. More antisub helicopters and planes are on the way, and they've got fighter cover. Our frigate will reach the galley in an hour. The battle group is heading toward the galley at flank speed. We've contacted a Greek destroyer, and they're joining us in two hours."

"Excellent, Admiral," his boss replied, immensely satisfied. "You've got that galley well protected obviously." The Admiral of the Sixth Fleet sighed with relief, and his staff, listening in on the speaker phone, sighed with him. They all realized that they'd just avoided a serious international incident.

"Yes, sir," Admiral Zimmerman replied. He hesitated. "Unless, of course, the sub aims to sink the galley. Right now, our antisub units aren't there yet, and we couldn't prevent that."

The men in the room stiffened with the shock of this news.

"Then it's still very serious, Admiral?" the Sixth Fleet Commander asked grimly.

"It is, sir, until the Russians contact their sub and call it off—before we have to fire on it."

"Stay on top of this, Admiral," the Fleet Commander said.

"Yes, sir," the admiral replied. On the bridge of the *Nimitz*, the tension was increasing.

The ominous international developments were not known to the people on the galley. What they did know was that the ship, its deck awash much of the time because it was heeling steeply, was tearing along at a great pace, rising and falling as it slashed its way through the seas of Ulysses. The huge Hawaiian was having a wonderful time. Penny and David were clustered around McPherson, holding on to lines and rails, absolutely exhilarated.

Ben didn't feel so well. His stomach was sending him strange signals and he didn't want to ignore them. "Better take in some sail, Mac," he said, as the boat slammed into another wave.

"Take in sail?" McPherson replied incredulously. "With a wind like this? Are you crazy?"

Ben wasn't crazy—he was sick. He rushed to the rail.

McPherson laughed his booming laugh and turned the wheel, increasing the wind's force against the speeding boat. The deck tilted even more. The foresail blew away, hanging in tatters of torn canvas that stuck straight out from the mast, pointing toward the black sky ahead.

McPherson laughed again. He loved it!

The helicopter pilot 100 yards away was shocked at the

galley's reckless race through the rough night waters. "That crazy McPherson's just blown away his foresail, sir," he radioed. "Looks like he's trying to tip over that boat!"

"Tell him to slow down before he sinks them all!" the frigate's captain yelled. "Tell him to take in sail." The captain turned to his exec. "He's crazy!"

"He's a sailor, Skipper," the exec replied with a grin. "He loves sailboats. I should have remembered that when he volunteered to go out there."

"Just so he doesn't sink the thing with all those Greek treasures! I'd lose my career!" the captain replied grimly. "He's playing sailboat while our battle group prepares to sink a Russian sub!"

On the submarine, miles away now, Captain Stokowski composed his message to Admiral Zukhov at the headquarters of the Black Sea Fleet. The captain was sick at heart. His boat was damaged but still moving. He'd spent a painful hour framing that short message. Finally, refusing to make excuses, he'd simply said that he aborted the mission rather than have his ship fired on by American warplanes.

"Code this," he ordered. Then he went to his cabin and waited for the admiral's reply. His thoughts were bitter. This was the end of his career, he knew. He'd failed to get those treasures. He'd made every effort, but he'd failed.

It seemed as if he'd been there just a few minutes when the orderly knocked on his door. "The message is ready, Captain."

Rising wearily, Stokowski left his cabin and entered the control room. He glanced at the instruments, then told the officer on deck, "Come to periscope depth. Prepare to send and receive signals. Call the men to battle stations. We don't know where those American planes are."

The sub's crew rolled out of their bunks and compartments and raced to their battle stations as the alarm sounded throughout the ship. Stokowski took over from the officer of the deck, and the sub began to ascend toward the surface.

"Periscope depth, Captain," the officer said.

"Stay there. Send the message."

In seconds the message was sent. Then a surprising number of messages began to come in to the men in communications. The captain frowned at the volume of signals. What could have happened. In a few minutes, he knew.

"From Moscow, sir," the communications officer said. "Navy headquarters. Admiral Jurginov commands you to ignore all previous orders and cease operations at once. Surface and call him immediately."

"Admiral Jurginov!" Captain Stokowski said, his jaw dropping. "What's going on?"

This was a calamity. Where was Admiral Zukhov of the Black Sea Fleet? He's the one who sent him on this mission. Why was Moscow going over his admiral's head like this?

"Bring the ship to the surface," he told the exec.

"There are more messages, Captain," the officer said.

"Just give me the substance of them." He couldn't take much more.

"Yes, sir. Admiral Jurginov has relieved Admiral Zukhov and has taken personal command of the Black Sea Fleet. He's ordered Badger bombers, armed, to search for us. They're to see that we don't approach that galley. They're to sink us if we do." The man's face was pale.

"Sink us!" the captain shouted. "Have they gone mad?"

"I don't know, sir. We're to acknowledge at once. At once, sir." The man was nervous as a cat—he didn't want their Badger bombers dropping missiles on them! Neither did the captain.

"Acknowledge. Tell them we ceased operations two hours ago. Tell them we're surfacing right away."

Now it wasn't his career Stokowski was worried about. It was his life.

CHAPTER 18

PENELOPE

So I thank you again, Admiral," Jurginov said to the Commander of the American Sixth Fleet. "We finally reached our sub. I had a long talk with its captain. He had been ordered to meet a catamaran and take on twelve barrels. He wasn't told what they contained, and didn't learn until the men who'd stolen them told him. The worst of it is that our admiral commanding the Black Sea Fleet was a part of this piracy. He'd sent the sub on that mission. And now he's escaped. But the assistant director of the Museum in Athens and his brother, who were on the galley, are now our prisoners on the sub! They're the ones who masterminded the theft and who pulled it off. I've been talking with the president of Greece and assured him we'll get these men back to him for trial."

"Congratulations, Admiral," the American officer replied. "That's wonderful cooperation. How can I thank you?"

"How can I thank *you*?" the Russian replied. "You saved our nation from a dreadful situation. The Greek president has been most understanding and is grateful to both of us for the return of his art treasures."

The waves of the sea were calmer as the sun rose above the horizon. But it was two hours later before Ben could rouse Mr. Spirodes from his drugged sleep. When the man was able to put his feet on the deck and sit on the bunk, he asked, "What happened?"

"You and your crewmen were drugged," Ben replied. "A lot happened after that, but why don't you drink some coffee first?"

Shocked, his eyes wide, Mr. Spirodes got to his feet, staggered, grabbed his head, and leaned against the wall. Then he recovered. "Let's get that coffee."

"The young lady made us a gallon," Ben said, as he led Mr. Spirodes to the kitchen. He poured him a mug of the steaming black liquid.

"Who's at the wheel?" Mr. Spirodes asked as he drank the scalding stuff, grimaced, then held out his cup for more.

"McPherson. He's the other medic. He's a real sailor, too, from Hawaii."

Mr. Spirodes downed his coffee. "Let's go!"

He bounded up to the deck, then raced to the quarterdeck where McPherson manned the wheel. As he climbed the steps, he looked seaward.

His astonished eyes beheld an American frigate sailing alongside just 300 yards to port. On the other side of the galley, a Greek frigate was pulling away and increasing speed. In the distance ahead, two big fighters swept toward them in tight formation. To the stern, a U.S. Navy helicopter hovered in the air.

"What's going on?" Mr. Spirodes asked, dumbfounded.

The big Hawaiian at the wheel laughed. "Captain, they say all good things come to an end. I've blown your foresail, but I've had a great time with this ship! What a magnificent vessel!"

"There's Mr. Spirodes!" Penny cried, as she turned and saw the skipper emerge from below. She, Mark, and David were forward, leaning against the rail, watching the navy ships. They rushed back to the stern. Penny ran up the steps to the quarterdeck and threw her arms around Mr. Spirodes's neck. "Oh, we're so glad you're awake, Mr. Spirodes!" she cried.

"What in the world happened?" the astonished man asked, as the three happy teenagers surrounded him.

"Well, sir," David replied, pointing, "that Greek frigate just took the barrels of stolen treasures from us. They're on their way to London."

"Stolen treasures?" Mr. Spirodes asked, stunned.

"The U.S. Navy Tomcats drove off that Russian submarine just as it was about to board us!" Mark added.

"Russian submarine?" Mr. Spirodes groped helplessly to untangle this news.

"And Carlos and Andropous Lycenus were the men who stole the Greek treasures and smuggled them aboard your ship," Penny added in a rush. "Lycenus is actually the blond sailor Carlos brought on board at the last minute. And he is Carlos's brother!"

"Lycenus was the man at the Athenian museum who disappeared," Mark reminded him. "The one that we saw on television when the barrels were taken from the museum to the ship, the man whose car we saw being dragged from the sea—he's the one who stole the ancient treasures from the museum."

"Good heavens!" Mr. Spirodes cried helplessly. "One thing at a time! I can't take all this in! First, haven't you three gone to bed at all?" he asked incredulously.

"We tried to around dawn, Mr. Spirodes," Penny replied, "but then those ships came and the boys wouldn't leave. So I stayed, too. I didn't want to miss anything!" *But she, does look tired,* David thought, as he gazed at her. *And I am too!*

"You should have seen those Tomcats strafe the Russian sub, Mr. Spirodes," David said. "We thought we'd be captured!"

"Strafe the Russian sub!" Mr. Spirodes asked, jaw dropping. "This is too much! Let me get some more coffee. Then you can start at the beginning!" Shaking his head in wonder, he went below for another mug.

Suddenly the two big Tomcats were right on them, flying low, waggling their wings as they flashed past. The men in the cockpits waved their hands at the teenagers. Mark, Penny, and David waved wildly back as the F-14s zoomed by, followed by their spectacular sonic booms!

"Boy! We owe them our lives!" Mark shouted through the noise, waving at the disappearing planes.

"Do you know how we can write and thank them, David?" Penny asked, eyes shining with excitement as the twin-engine fighters in tight formation zoomed up in a steep climb.

"I sure do! Carl and I write each other all the time. He's my cousin that I told you about who flies off the *Nimitz*. I'll give you his address—if you promise not to send him your picture!"

She smiled and blushed. "I promise!"

Mark laughed.

Just before the sun went down, Penny climbed the steps to the deck, feeling refreshed after hours and hours of sleep. Looking forward, she saw David leaning against the rail at the bow of the ship. She walked the length of the vessel, climbed the steps, and joined him.

"Hi!" she said suddenly behind his back.

He started, turned, and grinned when he saw her. "Hi! When did you wake up?"

She joined him at the rail. "Just a little while ago. I asked Mr. Spirodes to wake me in time to see the sunset."

David didn't tell her that he'd heard her ask Mr. Spirodes to wake her and had then done the same when she went below.

"Mark's still asleep," she said. "I peeked in his room."

David then asked the question that had been on his mind. "Penny, how in the world did you recognize Andropous Lycenus under that blond wig and behind that eye patch? If you hadn't done that, they would have stolen those Greek treasures!"

"Well, when I was little, I loved to see the photographs

Mom took. And I told her I wanted to take pictures like that. She taught me to look carefully at the things I saw, and to remember them. 'It's just a habit,' she said. 'You just have to practice it. Just practice looking, then remember what you see.' So I started doing that. It wasn't easy at first. But Mom kept encouraging me. And when I saw Lycenus on the ship, I knew I'd seen his face before. Then I remembered—it was on the television. It was the same face as the assistant director of the museum.

But, David, you understood their conversation! If you hadn't known German, you wouldn't have been able to understand what they were saying when we stood over their cabin window!"

"Well, that's funny," he said. "We lived in Germany for several years and that's where I learned the language. When we moved back to the U.S., though, I didn't want to be bothered with keeping up a foreign language. But Mom and Dad insisted. They got me a shortwave radio, and Dad and I listened to the 'Deutsche Welle.' That's Germany's international news program. Then it became fun. Anybody could do it if they wanted to. Boy, has it paid off today!"

He turned and looked at the lovely girl leaning against the rail beside him as the vessel plowed through the rough seas.

She glanced down at the paperback book in his hand. "What are you reading?"

"*The Odyssey*," he replied. "I got interrupted by all those shenanigans last night! Now I want to read the end again."

"Did it really take Ulysses ten years to get home from the

Trojan War?" she asked. Just the day before—it seemed like a year now—they'd been discussing the famous story.

"It really did. But the big thing is that his wife, Penelope, waited for him all that time. She waited ten years for the war to end and ten years for him to come home. A whole crowd of warriors camped on her estate, demanding that she marry one of them. But she kept putting them off for years and years, because she was faithful to her husband. She was an amazing woman."

"That's who I'm named for," Penny said thoughtfully. "Mom says that some of her friends didn't approve. They thought she should give all her children biblical names. But Dad said that the Lord gives us a lot of wonderful examples of character in human history. Dad likes the name Penelope because she was such a faithful wife. She waited for her husband to return, even when she didn't know he was still alive. Dad says that Mom is like that—faithful. And he tells me that I will be, too. That's what I pray for." She looked out to sea.

David gazed at her, standing close beside him, hair blown by the strong wind that swept across the bow of the ship. "Penny, I know you will."

Penny looked up at him for a long moment. He was very serious. Then she smiled.

Under a clear sky, the Greek war galley sailed smoothly through the seas of Ulysses.

Awesome Adventures With the Daring Family

Everywhere Mark and Penny Daring and their friend David go, there's sure to be lots of action, mystery and suspense! They often find themselves in the most unpredictable, hair-raising situations. Join them on each of their faith-building voyages in the *Daring Adventure* series as they learn to rely on each other and, most importantly, God!

Ambushed in Africa

An attempted kidnapping! A daring rescue! A breathtaking chase through crocodile-infested waters! Can the trio outwit the criminals before the top secret African diamond mine surveys are stolen?

Trapped in Pharaoh's Tomb

The kids are trapped in an ancient Egyptian tomb. How will they escape before the air runs out? Will they be able to outsmart their rival?

Stalked in the Catacombs

Penny, Mark and David explore Paris . . . but their adversary is lurking in the shadows. Will they be able to outrun him through the dark catacombs beneath the streets of the city?

Surrounded by the Cross Fire

Rival drug smugglers will stop at nothing to get what they want. Why are KGB agents following Penny? Will the kids get caught in the middle of the danger?

Hunted Along the Rhine

David, Mark and Penny are in Germany trying to foil a secret plot of the communists to gain control of the country. But someone's following them, watching their every move with a crossbow in hand!

Available at your favorite local Christian bookstore.